BLOODROSE HOUSE

BLOODROSE HOUSE

HOUSE

Cecily Crowe

ST. MARTIN'S PRESS
New York

FIC
CRO

5/85 B+7 7.59

Library of Congress Cataloging in Publication Data

Crowe, Cecily.
Bloodrose house.
I. Title.
PS3553.R59B6   1985   813'.54   84–23714
ISBN 0–312–08483–8

First Edition

10 9 8 7 6 5 4 3 2 1

For Dorothy Olding, with love and gratitude

· *I* ·

EVERYONE in Foxwold knew Bloodrose House was to let, so it was no surprise when word went out early in April that someone had taken it for six months. But when the lessee turned out to be a Mrs. Lucia Vail, an American lady staying at the Ravensmoor Arms, a writer no less (though a writer of what no one was sure), the event became all the more interesting.

She had been at the hotel for a week while she house-hunted and was recognizable in the village, particularly as it was the off-season and there were no other Americans about. She wouldn't have gone unnoticed anyway with her red-gold hair—natural, the women of Foxwold agreed, for her eyebrows were the same color and she had a few freckles on her cheekbones. She was youngish, thirtyish, husbandless (whether due to death or divorce it wasn't known), not tall but slim and smartly dressed, and Mr. Buckswick, proprietor of the hotel, gave her high marks for considerate behavior and prompt settling of accounts. Unfortunately, most of the time she looked preoccupied, or reserved, or melancholy—no one could find the precise word for it—a characteristic of writers perhaps, or widows, but it made her rather stony-faced, and it was only when she gave someone a rare smile that one realized how charming she could be.

In any case the villagers were intrigued that Mrs. Vail had chosen to settle for six months in Foxwold in the Yorkshire dales, and in Bloodrose House above all.

1

It had stood empty for more than a year and looked as if it would stand empty forever, and then Mr. Farr, the owner, whose life in a way was spent not letting valuable old property fall to pieces, suddenly ordered the house to be entirely renovated. Lady Quelling-Steele, an old family friend, did the decorating, driving all the way up from her Mayfair shop throughout the winter, and it was rumored in the pub at the Ravensmoor Arms that when the job was finished, her bill to Mr. Farr had put a decided blight on a budding affair. In the collective opinion of the villagers, who took a proprietary interest in Mr. Farr, a blight well worth the bill.

Still, everyone was thankful Bloodrose House had come to life, the windows no longer dark and empty like the eye-sockets of ghosts, but showing glimpses of Lady Quelling-Steele's lavishly draped chintzes, the trim repainted, the brass on the front door polished. The eerie flickering light, which one or two of the more indulgent regulars at the pub had claimed they saw in the front bedroom late at night, was seen no longer.

It wasn't a large house, but simple in a countrified Georgian style. Standing near the bottom of Church Street, which led gently downhill from St. Wilfred's church and the market square around the corner, it was one of a row of eighteenth-century houses built of buff-colored Yorkshire stone with white trim, separated from the paved path by their iron railings and a few steps. Opposite, across the street with its broad grassy verges and chestnut trees, there was a row of cottages of the same yellowish stone but much older and more rustic. The street ended at a turn onto a hump-backed bridge, where it meandered off into open farmland and the great looming rise of Ravensmoor.

By tradition, Bloodrose House belonged to the untitled second sons of the Viscounts Ravensmoor, to occupy or lease or let stand empty, but not to sell. But it was the work of humble bygone gardeners, loaned by bygone viscounts from their great manor on the other side of the moor, that gave the house its name. With the use of "settled water" and unspeakable fertilizers, they had nurtured the thorny stalks which clung to the mellow walls and produced a flaming mantle in June.

Even now, in April, the stalks were red. Blood red.

A BRISK breeze had cleared the sky, and the morning business of the village was in progress. Except on market day, parking was allowed in designated spaces in the open square. In the center the old-timers occupied their bench at the base of the Gothic war memorial (World War I), to converse in unintelligible Yorkshire dialect, while nearby a troop of helmeted young people, tall and spindly unlike their hulking American prototypes, admired each other's glittering motorcycles before rocketing off to a rally. Preoccupied farmers drew up in their four-wheel-drive vehicles and strode without a moment to spare to the bank or the ironmonger's. Women with shopping bags made their rounds from the old established butchers and greengrocers to the new superette. Mr. Buckswick swept the private parking space in front of the Ravensmoor Arms, an assortment of joined antique buildings, the oldest timbered black and white, which rambled across the north end of the square. A policeman, hands clasped behind his back, had stationed himself before the town hall, ready to chat with passersby and unobtrusively keep an eye on things.

The chimes of St. Wilfred's, dominating the town from a corner of the square adjacent to the Ravensmoor Arms, rang out the hour: It was time for elevenses, or coffee, a rite as firmly established as afternoon tea, and people were already turning into the snack bar or the health food restaurant or the lounge of the hotel.

Mrs. Vail, preparing for her move to Bloodrose House the following day, was traveling about the shops with a list and methodically loading her little red Mini, parked near the

3

monument. When she had pretty well completed her shopping, she stepped into the post office to see about having her mail delivered to the house, and Mr. Crouch gave her her morning's mail, which had just been sorted, rather than send it up to the hotel.

Quickly she ruffled through her letters—one from her mother in Bronxville, one from her editor, Henry Wetherwood, two heavy ones from her lawyer in New York (more papers to sign!), and a couple of bills—pocketed them, thanked Mr. Crouch, went out into the April sunlight, and there on the pavement, like a wind-up toy suddenly running down, stood stock still.

Passersby would have nodded to her had she not been so oblivious. Hands in the pockets of her burnt-orange wool coat, she stared with vacant eyes at the spire of the war memorial, and several people wondered if she might be plotting the next chapter of a book.

In fact, she was asking herself, When are you going to stop looking for a letter from *him?*

What do you expect? *Lucia, darling, it was all a mistake, I don't love her, I never loved her as much as you, tear up the divorce decree and let's start over together, All my love, Julian?*

Such lunacy, she well knew, only uncovered pain.

With an effort she roused herself, reburied the pain as a surgeon replaces folds of flesh, ground into self-counseling gear: The sooner she got back to work the better. She must look over Bloodrose House once more and put away her purchases, and then she would make her way to Ripon, where she might find typing materials not available in Foxwold. She would stop and ask Mr. Buckswick to put up a picnic lunch and seek out a fell or a moor on which to eat it.

She set herself in motion again.

MR. SLADE, estate agent for the Hon. Mr. Farr (Honourable with a *u)*, had shown her through Bloodrose House on a wet, dark afternoon, but the house was so bright with its fresh appointments, so much less gloomy than others she'd inspected, that she'd made up her mind instantly.

There was even something compelling about it. This is it, she felt: I must, I *must* have it!

Mr. Slade demurred at a six-month lease. He wanted to rent for at least a year; he would have to speak to Mr. Farr. But times were hard, the rent was high, the house too far from London to commute, and Mrs. Vail's was the first positive offer they'd had. With her neat solitary look, she was obviously not the sort to inflict wear and tear. Mr. Slade rang her up at the hotel to tell her Mr. Farr agreed to six months' occupancy.

Today, pausing as she unloaded staples from her car in the dancing shadows of budding chestnut trees, she discovered how handsome the house was in sunlight, with its graceful pediment over the black front door and a thick row of daffodils in the narrow bed behind the iron railings; how pretty the street, how pure and hopeful the air.

She was grateful then to Henry Wetherwood, her New York editor, for suggesting Foxwold, where he'd stopped once himself in pursuit of a roving poet, now in the outback of Australia. "The Brontë Museum in Haworth is only, what, half a day's drive away," Henry told her, for her work in progress was a novel based on the life of Charlotte Brontë.

Henry knew she needed to put distance between herself and Julian.

She was grateful, too, to her father for leaving her the wherewithal to make it possible. He had set up a trust fund Julian couldn't get his hands on—one *she* couldn't get her hands on, for Julian. Without it she would have had to go back to an office job. With it she would with care get by.

Foxwold, she was convinced this morning, was just the ticket.

Her eyes, sweeping past the cottages opposite, caught the slight movement of a curtain dropping. The furtiveness of it gave her a little start. But it was a small town, she reminded herself, and small towns were the same the world over. Even the English with their respect for privacy couldn't resist peeking at a newcomer.

"Ahoy there!"

She whirled about, further unsettled by this unlikely hail, to find a beetle-browed gentleman in knickerbockers plunging down the front steps of the house next door to hers, followed by a small shaggy beige dog stretching full length, fore and aft, as it sailed through the air between bounds.

"Luddington," the man told her, coming to attention before her and whistling through hairy nostrils, while his dog, halting at his heels, wagged up at him expectantly as if he were a never-failing source of delightful surprises. Although gray-haired, Luddington had black brows, prodigious to the point, possibly, of interfering with his vision, brows which glowered over nearly invisible deep-set eyes and a face full of weather-beaten seams and semicircles. "Will Luddington," he elaborated. "Some people call me Admiral. At your service."

It was easy to picture him barking orders from the bridge of a warship. But Lucia sensed he was the kind of powerful man who was a pushover for helpless women, or what he liked to think of as helpless women.

"Lucia Vail," she told him, trying to put out a hand from under the bundles piled under her chin.

"Allow me," he said, and carefully, without touching her breast, relieved her of her parcels.

Lucia, relinquishing them, understood that if the women he was a pushover for were not in fact helpless, he somehow rendered them so, for she felt all at once quite languid, a novel maidenly sensation. But he had stepped aside for her and she pulled herself together and went up her front steps and unlocked the door.

Not content with leaving her parcels on the hall table, he carried them back to the kitchen, where he set them down tidily on the new blue formica, and then went straight out to her car for more.

"There now," he said at last, taking a neat step backwards. "I'll leave you to your tasks. Shan't be a nuisance, you know, old bore next door always popping in, but you will call me if you need help, won't you?"

The eyes behind the bristling brows, she perceived, were the palest, brightest, most innocent blue. She broke into the smile that transformed her face, and he leaped to take the hand she offered, at once letting it go as if emotion might run away with him, and she saw him to the door.

"By the way," he said to her suddenly, "I'm having a few friends in for cocktails Friday, neighbors for the most part, you'll want to meet them and they'll want to meet you. Do come."

It was to be a healing period, this interlude in an out-of-the-way English village, far from sympathetic friends and reminders of Julian. She didn't intend to be a recluse exactly but she hadn't counted on cocktail parties with the neighbors. Indeed cocktail parties in general, particularly the hectic opportunistic parties of New York, were one of the things she'd fled from.

But Admiral Luddington had given her from beneath his hairy fringe an imploring glance, which he quickly averted lest it unfairly pressure her, and Lucia suspected he had invented the party on the spur of the moment. She accepted gracefully, and he gave a little whistling sigh through his nostrils.

There was a momentary pause as, with his hand on the door knob, the Admiral's gaze wandered over the roses of the sitting room wallpaper, visible from the hall.

"Glad to see the place occupied," he mused. "It should never have been abandoned as it was. Life deals one a blow now and then, it's to be expected, and a man must stand straight and go on."

Lucia had no idea what he was referring to, but she was

sure he himself had stood straight and gone on, in war and peace.

In an incomprehensible sequitur he added, "Never married, myself." He opened the door. "Friday at six then, but in the meantime I am always at your call." He snapped his fingers for the eager little dog quivering outside. "Come, Bertie," he commanded, as if Bertie might have a mind to do otherwise, and marched down the steps, the dog sailing through the air beside him. Up the steps next door they went and into their own house.

Lucia turned about, glancing again at the window across the street. She had the feeling again that she was being watched.

She closed her door, hung up her coat, returned to the kitchen and began putting away her supplies.

So, according to the Admiral, someone had suffered a blow in Bloodrose House. Who? she wondered. What sort of blow? And what did it have to do with marriage?

Perhaps an intuitive sense of this tragedy, whatever it was, accounted for her compelling decision to rent. Perhaps the house had given off sympathetic vibrations—one survivor of blows to another.

Sunlight filled the windows, framed in blue-checked curtains. All the modern appliances sparkled. Lucia looked forward to pottering about in this kitchen, for under her New York facade there was an inborn domestic bent.

You and I—she communed, so to speak, with the house—are starting over.

And someday she might ask the Admiral what had happened, why the house had been abandoned, for she was sure to get to know him better. He was too nice to be a bore.

Julian, now (ungovernably her thoughts still homed in on Julian), could never be called a bore, but neither would anyone call him nice. Julian simply was not especially nice.

Aghast, she halted in her work, arms upraised as she stocked the cupboard shelves, a trace of a smile on her lips.

Even her father had never said "Julian is not nice." Unreliable, yes, irresponsible, and self-centered, which at the time she'd translated in her besottedness into driven, frustrated, and searching (she had expected fatuously to be the answer to his search), but nothing so concise and belittling as "not nice."

A truant giggle escaped her, a sound she hadn't heard from herself in a long time. There was a lot of relief in a giggle. And a lot of guilt. For she found it hard to lower the banner of loyalty to Julian, to surrender not only loyalty but her own self-deception.

Once more she took herself in hand, finished in the kitchen, and embarked on a closer inspection of the house.

A pantry door opened into a small white-paneled dining room with windows on the street, a little bandbox with a crystal chandelier and yellow-striped draperies, perfect for small dinner parties. But dinner parties large or small, like cocktail parties, didn't figure in Lucia's plans, and quietly she closed the door and crossed the hall.

The sitting room, or as Mr. Slade called it, the lounge, running from the front of the house almost to the back, was a bower of roses. Heavily draped and ball-fringed curtains of rose-printed chintz dragged extravagantly on the cream-colored carpet, rose-covered sofas faced each other across the Georgian fireplace, tufted Victorian chairs bursting with roses abounded, and the walls were papered with redder and yet more exuberant blooms. The effect was somewhat dizzying but far from dreary. The decorator, Lady Somebody-Somebody, mentioned by Mr. Slade, knew what she was about.

Behind the sitting room at the back of the house there was a small study, with French doors opening on the rear garden. It had been painted dove-gray with white trim, and there was just room enough for a flat desk and chair of beautiful old wood, an easy chair by a little marble-faced hearth, and inset bookcases with arched moldings.

Mrs. Berry, who cleaned and who, as Mr. Slade had stated unequivocally, went with the house at the tenant's expense, (Mr. Farr provided the once-a-week gardener), had laid a coal fire in the grate, ready to be lit. The easy chair faced a view of the garden. Like the kitchen, the study was full of sunlight. Here, Lucia knew, she would spend most of her time.

Next, with an armful of tissues and soaps, she went up the gracefully curving staircase.

There were only two bedrooms, a spare room with sloping eaves overlooking the back garden, decorated demurely in a pretty Liberty print, and a larger, grander one overlooking the street. Between them, where once there had probably been another bedroom, there was now a spacious bathroom.

Having disposed of soaps and tissues, Lucia approached the large mauve and moss-green master bedroom she supposed she would occupy. Doubtfully she eyed the big bed. On the wall over the padded headboard, taffeta draperies were arranged to fall from a crown topped with a gilt cupid. A bed obviously meant for connubial bliss.

Would a single woman, she asked herself, find this a comfortable place to spend her nights?

Between the two front windows a mirrored dressing table, swathed in taffeta skirts, seemed to cry out for oversized bottles of My Sin and Joy. Experimentally Lucia seated herself before the mirror.

She had lost weight in the past few months and her cheekbones were more pronounced. She wore less makeup than she did in New York, and she hadn't bothered to cover the scattering of freckles on the upper curve of her cheeks or darken the gold-brown brows and lashes. Her skin, more taut now, had a transparency, a smoothness, as if anguish had given her a kind of face-lift, erasing a layer of disguise, leaving the gray-green eyes wider, brilliant with aftershock; a convalescent face.

In fact, in this erotic setting she looked like a postulant nun, and she made a grimace and turned about. No one so badly burned and twice-shy, so undeniably retired from the sexual arena, would rest easily in such a room, and she decided then to use the chaste but cozier spare room over the garden.

Mrs. Berry had lined the dresser drawers, hung sachets in the wardrobes and put out fresh towels; everything was dusted, laundered, waxed, or polished. Their paths hadn't yet crossed but already Lucia had a high regard for her. There was nothing more to be done. Tomorrow she would have only to move her bags from the hotel, unpack them, and go to work.

She went down to the kitchen again and put on her coat, but on an impulse she opened the back door into the walled garden and stepped outside.

An oak tree spread feathery buds over a lawn thick and flat as carpeting. Daffodils bloomed in knife-edge beds bordering the old brick walls, and neatly tended plants promised displays to come.

A bench and a rustic table and chairs were set out under the great tree, and Lucia sat down for a minute to enjoy the sun and air. An invisible robin, the small English robin, spun a silvery thread of song somewhere nearby.

There was a warmth in the enclosure and a welcome. She looked up at the gleaming windows, the yellow-brown stone covered with thorny red branches. All houses had secrets, and Bloodrose House had a right to its share.

You will be better off when you leave than when you arrived.

She made this pronouncement in silence to herself, but she heard it as if from the house and its stillness, its air of waiting for her.

She felt at home.

She became aware of the unyielding bulge in her coat pocket and realized she hadn't read her mail. She could at least open her mother's letter here in this pleasant garden.

11

Her mother was diminutive in size but formidable in strength of character. Widowed seven years, blonde, fastidious, and sensible, in demand for luncheon and bridge parties, steadfast in volunteer work, she was a person of great calm and restraint. She couldn't have been surprised at the breakup of Lucia's marriage but she had never said so, nor did she utter a word of remonstrance when Lucia decided to remove herself to North Yorkshire.

Lucia dear:
    I'm glad to hear you've finished your "homework" at the British Museum concerning C. Brontë, and find Foxwold to your liking. I really get a thrill out of your adventure! Unlike me, you have been willing to break out of a safe, conventional background, and your life is much more interesting than mine!

Interesting indeed, thought Lucia. If life with the glamorous Julian had taught her anything, it was that for all her escape from a safe, conventional background she had inherited inescapably her parents' old-fashioned standards.

    People don't try so hard *not* to be different these days, as they did in mine, and that is healthy! Perhaps the fact that Julian is remarried now, which of course you must have heard, will free you from any lingering doubts. Anyway, I wish you well in Foxwold, and if I can do anything for you here, if you need something from Bloomingdale's for instance . . .

But the letter had blurred and sunk to Lucia's lap.
So he had married her.
She hadn't heard. None of her friends would have wanted to be the first to tell her.
Rather than a sense of freedom she felt a draining away, a drastic mental and physical revision which cooled her brain and proceeded downward over shoulders, arms and legs,

hands and feet, rendering them transparent and inoperative. It might be the way a person feels awakening in a recovery room to find the dreaded amputation has taken place.

Her mother had carefully crossed out a word before *doubts*. Perhaps it was *hopes*.

For a long while Lucia sat there, merely breathing.

She *had* hoped.

She looked at the yellow house. It was different now. It had been a house, she realized, in which she would have lived with hope, and now it was one in which she would live without.

You see, the house seemed again to speak to her through herself: *The lesson begins. Healing can be painful, too.*

Stand straight and put the past behind you, the Admiral had said. Lesson for the day.

She got heavily, clumsily, to her feet.

She went inside, locking the garden door behind her, went through the house and out the front.

A woman with dyed black hair was sweeping the walk of the house opposite, the same house where the curtain had twitched. Mechanically Lucia gave her a nod and a half-wave and groped for the handle of her car door.

The woman turned her back and kept on sweeping.

Vaguely, without really penetrating her numbness, this struck Lucia as unfriendly.

"DON'T miss the 'all," Mr. Buckswick advised her, handing over a neat carton containing her picnic lunch.

"What hall, Mr. Buckswick?" She'd improved at translating his unaspirated words ever since his warning on her arrival not to go up the steep 'ill to the top of Ravensmoor in low gear, as the roadside signs suggested, lest her car over-'eat. He was a burly, rusty-haired man, partial to houndstooth checks, with that Englishman's trait of carrying a lot of unassailable moral weight under a genial exterior.

"Why, Farthing," he told her. "Lord Ravensmoor's residence. It's not open to visitors even though 'is Lordship lives in the south of France, but you can catch a glimpse of it as you come down off the moor. Look sharp to your right and you'll see it nestled in the 'ollow."

She took his advice and drove up over Ravensmoor, its heather, not yet in bud, making a rusty cover for rabbits and grouse, while a hawk wheeled overhead; a wild and desolate place which never failed to give her a little feeling of dread. Then, descending at last into the rolling dales, dotted with ewes and newborn lambs, she did glimpse over a high wall a long Tudor pile of bronze-tinged stone. She stopped the car and backed up to pinpoint it again.

Farthing. There wasn't a sign of life about it, although the grounds were carefully manicured. It slept in the sun on its velvet lawns a quarter of a mile away, a treasure of a place.

Lucia was beginning to understand the reassurance in centuries-old dwellings, the visible and tangible fact that the net result of the ups and downs of life was peace.

Lucia in fact, quietly and alone, was reading lessons in many things once ignored or taken for granted.

The Ravensmoor family, judging by the Hall and the hotel's name and the effigies in St. Wilfred's church, had exerted considerable influence in the region for a long time.

She drove on at last in search of an attractive spot for lunch. The paved road curved away out of the dale, but a narrow unpaved lane led invitingly deeper into it. Sighting in the distance a stream and great sheep-mown fells, she turned into the lane. Soon she came upon a closed gate barring her way, but it wasn't locked, and since there was no sign of habitation where she could ask permission to pass through it, and as the scenery in the distance grew ever more glorious, she decided to continue, being careful to close the gate behind her.

There were two more gates to open and close, and her temerity wavered, but after the third gate she was in the dale, and there she found a sheltering bank in the sun, facing

14

the stream. She pulled the car off the lane, got out her lunch and a raincoat to sit on, and made herself comfortable with her back against the bank.

Sheep nibbled unconcernedly around her, and handsome black-and-white lapwings foraged. Along the banks of the stream below there were yellow drifts of daffodils, and beyond the stream the fells rose in soft blue-green flanks, mounting to the dark crown of a moor.

The purity of the air, fragrant with earth and grass and that distilled essence of high places, was infinitely soothing, and Lucia, working her way through Mr. Buckswick's overly generous lunch, felt this was a country she could lose herself in and not feel lost.

But fate, with its lesson for the day, hadn't finished belaboring her.

A farmer drove up in a Land-Rover, sharply pointed out she was trespassing on private land, gave her permission to finish her lunch but implied she had then better take herself off and not return so presumptuously, and drove on.

It was the last straw. Two great tears filled her eyes and rolled down her cheeks. She gathered up her things and got back into her car.

There was no escape, really, anywhere.

The rug under one was never secure. There would always be samples of paradise and there would always come a time to be thrown out.

There would always be divorcées in tears.

She had to laugh, then, savingly, at the woeful spectacle of herself. She mopped her cheeks with her sleeve and headed out of the dale for Ripon and stationery supplies.

· *II* ·

LUCIA moved into Bloodrose House the next day. Mr. Buckswick followed in his little van to lend a hand with her luggage. A cold wind blew off the moors, and sunlight alternated with wild showers of rain.

As Lucia moved to insert her key in the lock, the door was opened by a tiny pallid beak-nosed woman with shoe-button eyes. "Welcome!" she croaked.

"Mrs. Berry?" Lucia inquired, taken aback. From the evidence of unstinting industry about the house she had imagined a strapping Yorkshire woman with apple cheeks. Mrs. Berry was more like a pint-sized witch.

"Aye, it is!" Mrs. Berry stepped back and opened the door wide. "Come in and make yourself at home!"

Behind her on the hall table blazed a bouquet of freshly picked daffodils, and an auspicious aroma of homemade soup leaked from the kitchen, both wonderfully reassuring on a cold and blustery day. Lucia gave her her warmest smile and put out her hand to grasp a timid little bundle of bones.

"Take them straight upstairs!" commanded Mrs. Berry, spying the innkeeper waiting on the steps with Lucia's bags. "The front bedroom!"

"The back bedroom," put in Lucia.

"Back bedroom!" barked Mrs. Berry, like a mini-sergeant-major. Timid my eye, thought Lucia.

Mr. Buckswick lugged bags, typewriter, and various tote bags containing overflow to their appointed places, saw to the adapter for the electric typewriter, and then went about testing thermostat and switches. "Mr. Farr's Lady Q. knew her job," he declared, "no matter 'ow 'igh 'anded!"

"You sing out, luv," he said at the door, absolutely refusing a tip, "if you need anything." Now that they were no longer on a commercial footing, he felt free to address her in the friendly countrified way. "And pay us a visit once in a while at the 'otel."

A white Mercedes was drawn up in the street, and as Lucia and Mr. Buckswick stood on the front steps, two elderly ladies emerged from the house next door, on the other side from the Admiral's house, one on each arm of a fair-haired young man in smartly cut clothes, and made for the car. They were all three laughing as if relishing something said indoors a moment before, but when they spied Lucia, the ladies, clutching hats and scarves and capes which lifted in the wind, hallooed a welcome, and the young man gave her a half-nod, half-bow. He then devoted his attention to seating the ladies in the Mercedes, tucking in tag ends of scarves and capes, and finally, with a last smile for Lucia, got in himself and drove sedately away.

"The Misses Ambrose," informed Mr. Buckswick. "Miss Adelaide, the 'eavier one, is eighty-five, and the other, Miss Olivia, with the white 'air, is ninety. Sharp as tacks and lively as monkeys. Miss Adelaide taught me maths at Foxwold School. That's their great-nevoo from York, 'e's done well in the antiques business, comes up regular to take them out to lunch and such, 'though it's my opinion that if 'e were pitted against them in an endurance contest, the old girls would win 'ands down."

"Who lives across the street?" asked Lucia. "Directly across from here?"

Mr. Buckswick's florid face assumed a judicial look. "That would be Miss Morgan. You've seen 'er, 'ave you? She keeps to 'erself." He pursed his lips, suggesting it was his policy as an innkeeper not to gossip, a suggestion not entirely based on fact. "She's 'ad 'er troubles. There now, I'll be off." His glance rose from Lucia's face to the stone facade above her. "If anyone can, you'll bring luck to this 'ouse." And he too departed.

"Unpack a bit," decreed Mrs. Berry, "and I'll fix your lunch by the fire before I go."

And so at length Lucia found herself in the study at a little table beside a glowing coal fire, dipping up hearty oxtail soup. A magenta gloxinia bearing the Admiral's card brightened the room, and beyond the French doors sunlight suddenly replaced rain. Lucia's typewriter, fresh paper, notebooks, and manuscript waited on the desk nearby.

She felt far from qualified to bring good luck to house or human, but if appreciation generated a favorable breeding ground, luck might follow. With the Admiral on one side and the jolly Misses Ambrose on the other, she felt buttressed by good will. And truth to tell, the admiring smile of the fair-haired great-nephew had done nothing to cloud her contentment.

She pitied Miss Morgan across the street. Living alone with a feeling of friendliness wasn't so bad, but living alone without it must be hell.

SHE worked all afternoon, stopping only to replenish the fire, whose care and feeding Mrs. Berry had painstakingly explained. The Brontë girls had worked in their father's parlor in the same blustery Yorkshire weather; Lucia felt immeasurably closer to them than in New York or London, and her writing deepened with a greater sympathy. This was her fourth book, and despite the fact that Julian had called them hysterical romances, each one was better than the last, and both she and her editor felt she was hitting her stride.

At five she got up to ease her back and turn on the electric teakettle. While waiting for it to boil she telephoned the Admiral to thank him for the gloxinia.

"Hope it doesn't clash with that woman's decor!" he bawled, as if through a megaphone across a watery waste. "Getting settled in, are you? Looking for you Friday, you know. Kind of you to call!"

She was preparing her mug of tea when she heard the front door open and shut. "Who's that?" she cried, hurrying out to the hall. She thought she'd left the automatic lock on.

A tall, thin woman with a mass of frosted ash-blonde hair stood unwrapping herself from a voluminous mauve silk rain cape. She had an unlined, worked-on face which indicated she was older than she looked, and pale, glacial, beautifully made up eyes that fastened upon Lucia, sweeping her up and down.

"I didn't hear you knock," exclaimed Lucia, more in astonishment than rebuke.

"Quelling-Steele," said the woman, as if that explained everything, and perhaps it did. Speak of the devil, Lucia told herself; this, then, was the decorator whom the Admiral had called That Woman. "May I come in," she said, with a descending intonation intended to remind one of one's manners rather than ask a question.

And Lucia, forbearing to answer "But you *are* in," quickly stepped aside to show the lady into the sitting room.

Lady Quelling-Steele was not to be hurried. "So *you* rented the place," she said, as without invitation she continued stripping things off and flinging them down on a hall chair. Driving gloves and a scented Hermes scarf followed her cape. She wore a mauve cowl-necked cashmere sweater over a mauve suede skirt, long and full and supple as silk, with suede boots to match, and from her thin neck and wrists hung a tinkling collection of chains and exotic, cumbersome charms. "American," she pronounced, like a judgment, still giving Lucia the once-over. "I can tell by the, humm, clothes."

The humm clothes didn't sound in any way complimen-

19

tary, and confronted with such total elegance Lucia, too, gave low marks to her own shapeless wool cardigan and corduroy slacks.

Lady Quelling-Steele pursed her frosted mauve lips and sucked in her cheeks. "I expect Tony took one look at you and gave his consent."

"To what?" asked Lucia, befuddled.

"To a six-month lease."

"Oh. You mean Mr. Farr." Lady Quelling-Steele was certainly well informed about Bloodrose House. "I haven't met him."

"Oh?" The suppressed smile vanished. "Oh, well, then." The cold eyes looked colder still. "I expect you will." She strode past Lucia and entered the sitting room.

It had darkened outside with another shower. "Let me light some lamps," said Lucia, hastening after her.

"Don't bother. I shan't be staying, actually." She caught sight of Lucia's writing paraphernalia spread over the desk in the study and marched across the carpet. She put her nose in the study door and then whirled about, again with her version of barely contained mirth. "Don't *tell* me you're a scribbler?"

Lucia shifted inner gears. She could perhaps give leeway to a person who needed to minimize one's clothes, but like a protective mother she would not permit belittling of her work.

"I'm a writer, yes," she said quietly and firmly. "Will you sit down a moment?"

"No. I've been sitting for hours, coming up from London. I'm stopping overnight at the Arms with my assistant, actually, on our way to a client in Newcastle. Poor Rodney, he hates being left to himself." She went over to the mantel and rearranged the Chinese porcelain, then executed another of her whirling turns, like a leading lady on a stage. "I should stay clear of Tony Farr if I were you. If you know what's good for you."

Lucia's jaw dropped. But it was pathetic, really—the scathing voice, the haggard face. Was it the bitterness of an older woman confronting a younger one? *Something* was eating her alive. Lucia wouldn't have been surprised if Lady Quelling-Steele already knew Lucia was American, single, and a writer, and had made this stop in Foxwold to see for herself.

The sympathy in Lucia's eyes only served to thwart the lady the more. She thrust out her chin and made for the hall, bangles jingling, snatched up her things and wrenched open the door.

She paused on the threshold as Lucia caught up with her. A sleek silver car stood in the street below.

"One might enjoy oneself in Bloodrose House, I suppose," she said, facing about to Lucia, "but *do* be careful. It's *not* a happy house, you know. I did my best to improve the atmosphere but there are some things one can't paper over. I *hope* you're a good sleeper."

With these cheerless hints she turned and went down the steps.

Lucia, having made sure the safety latch was on, returned to the kitchen. She shook her head. She'd made an enemy without even trying. Any unhappiness involved in living in Bloodrose House couldn't compare, she was certain, with the ordeal of living inside Lady Quelling-Steele.

And what was all that about Tony Farr?

IN FACT, Lucia was a good sleeper, now that the worst was over with Julian.

But in the middle of the night she was awakened by a cry.

She sat bolt upright. Her bedside clock said five minutes past three.

The cry seemed to come from the front of the house. Had she dreamed it? It was a cry of heartbreak. She put on the light, grabbed her robe, ran to the front bedroom, and peered out at the street. Clouds tumbled across the sky, passing over a quarter moon, and the branches of the chestnut trees made pulsating veins against the silver light. She opened the window and the cold rushed at her face and throat.

"Is anybody there?" she called.

The wind sighed in the swaying branches. Not a light shone anywhere. There were bushes at each corner of Bloodrose House, screening the path, but Lucia didn't think anyone lurked behind them.

An owl, no doubt.

She closed the window and went back to bed. Strange: in New York there were hoots and shouts and backfires and siren wails all night long, and she never turned a hair.

Perhaps she'd had a nightmare, dreaming fruitlessly of Julian. It wouldn't be the first time.

She had strong intuitions, responding to people in ways they never dreamed of, to places also, a constant sensory tuning-in that was part of her makeup as a writer. But she could not and would not believe in ghosts. Even if Lady Quelling-Steele wanted her to.

If you hear a voice calling "Heathcliff!" she told herself, you're in trouble.

She read a little while and slept again. The desolate cry was not repeated.

· III ·

THE wind dropped overnight, and the morning sky was a cool, vaporous blue. It was market day, and by nine o'clock the square was crowded with stalls shaded by gaudily striped awnings and laden with choice fruits and vegetables, fish, flowers, sweets, plants, costume jewelry, towels, china, leather goods, baskets, shoes, books, and so on. It looked like a carnival, but in fact market day was serious business, and the square droned with purposeful chatter as the townspeople, shopping bags in hand, some with well-behaved dogs on leashes, made their transactions. A large van from the National Blood Transfusion Service was drawn up opportunely before the town hall, and the coffee bars were thriving.

Lucia walked up to the square after breakfast with her own shopping bag. She'd explored the market the previous week when she was staying at the Arms, and she now made her way to a favorite fruit stall at the north end of the square, where she bought bananas without blemish, small manageable pineapples, and translucent seedless grapes shaped like zeppelins. She'd planned to go straight home then to work, but because the sky was so bright and the mood of the market so jaunty, she dallied awhile looking for temptation—a small treasure at the antiques stall, perhaps, or a rare mystery among the paperbacks.

"Mrs. Vail, Mrs. Vail," called a voice in an Old Testament sing-song, "good morning!"

It was the rector of St. Wilfred's, a lanky, sandy-haired

man whose hand Lucia had shaken after last Sunday's service. At the altar his voice could drop into a full-bodied baritone and in the pulpit it could be penetrating, with bugle-notes. His incantation of her name was sung in a reedy oboe-like tenor.

"Good morning, Mr. Goodfriend." *His* name was unforgettable, but Lucia was impressed that a man almost studiously helter-skelter could remember hers.

"Are they not beautiful?" he fluted, holding up a pair of sandals, which Lucia thought quite hideous. "Would not the disciples have coveted them? That is, if they coveted anything?" He swayed and pivoted as he sang, his mousy hair falling over his brow; his clerical collar was too big for him, his gray suit flapped on his bony frame. But Lucia discerned a canniness behind his steel-rimmed spectacles and suspected the eccentric-clergyman act was a camouflage for astutely operating powers of observation, the sandals a ploy to hold her attention. In other words, while singing and swaying he was engaged in subtle sizing-up. "Would they, I wonder," he went on, and the woman in charge of the stall wore a patient smile, "would they be considered too 'far-out' for a country cleric?"

"Yes," replied a short sturdy woman in brown tweeds, imperturbably examining footwear behind him. "Put them back, Cedric. The fashion of this world passeth away." She turned, smiled at Lucia, came forward and thrust out a hand. "Hello, I'm Peg Goodfriend." Her grip was firm and decisive. "You're our new neighbor. Delighted to meet you. How are you getting on at Bloodrose House?"

While they conversed, Lucia thought, really, it seemed as if the mismatched couples of the world generated the strongest bond between them. Peg Goodfriend, a keen terrier of a woman joined to an Afghan hound of a man, had a look of honesty and peace, and flighty Cedric, happily kept within bounds, had all the scope he desired. Together they gave off an impression of interdependent freedom.

A teen-aged apparition in a costume about as far-out as anything Lucia had seen in Britain—and teen-aged Brits, she'd decided, could be farther-out than their contemporaries in the States ever dreamed of being—wandered over from another booth and was introduced as the Goodfriends' daughter, Iris, further confirming Lucia's belief in the Goodfriends' live-and-let-live policy.

Short like her mother and well-rounded, the girl wore a collection of drab skirts and sweaters, the short-sleeved ones over the long-sleeved ones, thick woolly green leg-warmers, and low-heeled gold slippers. Her make-up was flour-white and crimson, and she had somehow made her hair stand on end in points like a fright wig. She had adorable ears and a fragile neck, and she gave Lucia a soft little hand and in a childlike voice uttered the single word, "God," but whether as an affirmation of faith or an exclamation of dismay, Lucia had no way of knowing.

"See," cried the rector, capturing his daughter's arm and pointing out the sandals, "see what your mother forced me to renounce!"

"Oh, Daddy, *God*," said Iris, who though limited in vocabulary had a sweet way about her, and laughing, they set to perusing the shoes together.

Iris was learning to teach nursery children, her mother told Lucia confidently, and Lucia entertained a picture of Iris in this get-up at a conference with goggle-eyed parents. Peg then wound up the conversation, promising to call when Lucia was settled. "Please let us help if we can. The rectory is at the top of the hill opposite the church, and we are always available."

She fell suddenly silent, eyeing Lucia in a way that meant she would probably add something when she'd formulated her thoughts, and Lucia, waiting, guessed the kind of remark it would be, for it was becoming eerily familiar. "Yes," said Peg, as if in answer to Lucia's guess, "you're just the right person for Bloodrose House." She smiled, coming out of her abstraction. "Ghosts and curses, flickering lights in the windows, and so on are for the romanticists, don't you think, but a house does take on something from its occupants. You'll brighten it, I know!"

They parted cordially, the Reverend Goodfriend making a bow as though doffing a plumed hat and Iris showing a dimple under her white paint, and they went their separate ways.

Homeward bound, Lucia took the path through the church-yard rather than going round by the pavement. There was a fragrance of dense holly and boxwood here, and the centuries-old gravestones created a world apart, appropriate to Lucia's reflections, which had returned to ghosts and curses. Presumably, according to Peg's implication, others in Foxwold did believe in them. Presumably, ghosts and curses had been rumored in connection with Bloodrose House.

She was now of two minds about tracking down what, if anything, had happened to give rise to these rumors. It didn't matter; or rather, she didn't want it to matter. The house was hers now, she felt at home in it, she didn't want any insidious rumors upsetting her first tenuous contentment. Not dwelling on the past was part of her own therapy and should be therapy for Bloodrose House, too.

But what about the anguished cry in the night?

The memory of it rested in the back of her mind like a stone, cold, weighty, unexplained.

SHE went down the path on the far side of the church to a lych-gate and, emerging at the top of Church Street, came upon the Misses Ambrose, the elderly ladies who lived next door, also returning from market but approaching from around the churchyard on the pavement. They greeted Lucia as if they were old friends, although it was the first time they'd actually met.

Miss Adelaide, gray-haired, with rough-hewn features

and a powerful voice, stouter and younger than Olivia, was spokesperson for the two but deferred constantly and affectionately to her sister. Olivia, she said, was going home to bake apple tarts, she'd send one round to Lucia, she made the best apple tarts in Foxwold, if not in all of North Yorkshire; and white-haired Olivia smiled a gentle smile.

"Olivia's the homemaker of the family," boomed Adelaide as they moved down the broad path together. "There were nine of us, all obstreperous, and Olivia took care of us and our Dad so that we could go out and make careers for ourselves. When Dad died I told Olivia it was time she pleased herself—travel, go to school to learn a vocation, move to town, whatever she liked, and we'd back her, for she deserved it. But do you know, of her own free will she elected to go on keeping house. Didn't you, Olivia?"

"Yes, dear, I did," replied Olivia softly, and Lucia sensed that Olivia had as much wisdom as her obstreperous brothers and sisters.

"Only the two of us at home now," continued Adelaide, "but we keep lively, we're always on the go." She gave way to a gust of laughter. "We've a friend who's just turned seventy, but imagine, she's decided she's old! Takes to her bed every afternoon at four! Doesn't she, Olivia?"

"Yes, dear, she does."

"*Seventy,* mind you!" scoffed Adelaide, the eighty-five-year-old.

"You taught school, Mr. Buckswick told me," said Lucia. "You taught him mathematics?"

"Ho, yes, that nice lad. Yes, there were at one time very few in Foxwold I *didn't* teach." Another peal of laughter escaped her. "Every now and then a bald gentleman with a paunch rushes up to me, asking plaintively, 'Miss Ambrose, don't you remember me? You taught me!' Well, of course I don't remember them all, there were hundreds of them! But I always say I do, dear things."

She had been one of those teachers, Lucia was positive,

who shine like beacons in one's early life, and mathematics learned from Miss Ambrose would be mathematics learned forever.

A car had drawn up some distance ahead of them, and a slender brown-skinned man got out, bearing a black medicine bag, and crossed to one of the very old houses opposite Bloodrose, a house with a small sign half-buried in ivy stating the doctor's name and surgery hours, which Lucia had noticed earlier.

"Morning, Dr. Jenna!" called Adelaide. He waved a thin brown hand, and they watched him proceed indoors.

"Charming fellow," declared Adelaide as they moved on down the street. "He's done wonders for Olivia's arthritis, hasn't he, Liv?"

"Yes, dear, he has."

"But 'the Mysterious East,'" informed Adelaide, "is not an idle phrase. Indians *are* mysterious. Dr. Jenna's head *cannot* be filled with exotic dreams, but somehow he gives that impression. Plays cricket, goes to chamber concerts, has a respectable housekeeper, is thoroughly intelligent and conscientious: yet he *is*, in my private opinion, *mysterious*."

Lucia tried not to smile as Adelaide's private opinion carried up and down Church Street. Miss Morgan, tidying her front walk again, looked up at the sound.

"But if you should need a physician, Mrs. Vail," interjected Olivia, "which I hope you never do, you couldn't ask for a better man."

"Thank you for recommending him. And won't you please call me Lucia?"

"Right you are," agreed Adelaide, "and you must call us Adelaide and Olivia. Hullo, Miss Morgan!"

This salutation caught the black-haired woman just as she was ducking indoors with her broom. It was fairly obvious to Lucia that she wished to avoid the three approaching women, but either Adelaide didn't notice or chose to ignore it.

Miss Morgan turned in her doorway with a trapped, catlike expression, her small pale eyes bright as diamonds. She might have been attractive once, but the unrelieved blackness of her hair and a heavy application of eye-liner hardened her face. "H'lo," she squeezed out between thin lips. Again she moved to go indoors, and again Adelaide detained her.

"You've met our new neighbor, Mrs. Vail?"

The thin mouth twisted slightly; it could have been a smile or a sneer. "Haven't had the pleasure," she said, giving a nod in Lucia's direction, and then she did escape, and her door closed.

Exaggeratedly Adelaide pulled her mouth to one side as if to speak *sotto voce,* which she was quite incapable of doing. "Not the sociable sort, as you'll have observed," she said, steering them across the street to Bloodrose House. "Too bad. She's been a good lady's maid, a good nurse, and she's had her ups and downs. Still, I don't countenance bad manners; never did and never shall."

Miss Morgan, thought Lucia, more than being ill-mannered gave an impression of bright-eyed, thin-lipped unbalance. "I wondered if it was just Americans she didn't like."

Adelaide shrugged. "Oh, well, she may resent anyone but the Farr family occupying Bloodrose House." Why? Lucia wanted to ask, but Adelaide wheeled about, cutting short any more talk about Miss Morgan. "And here we are! We must run, Olivia wants to make her tarts, and then we're meeting a friend in Harrogate for lunch, thank God I still have my driver's license. What luck to fall in with you like this! Comfortable here, are you? All's well?"

All's well but a terrible cry in the night, Lucia had an impulse to say, but didn't. It was no time to stir up a fuss, too cheery a morning even to give credence to such a cry.

"All's well. I'm fortunate in my neighbors."

"So are we. We'll see you at Will Luddington's party on Friday."

"Yes, I've been invited."

"I thought as much, since you're the guest of honor!" And Adelaide's shout of laughter ricocheted off the thorn-laced facade of the house. "Simon's coming, our great-nephew. He wouldn't miss a chance to meet you. 'What a smashing girl!' he said the other day, at sight of you. Goodbye then, until Friday. We'll leave a tart for your lunch."

"Goodbye, dear," murmured Olivia. "Let us know if we can do anything for you."

Lucia ran lightly up the steps.

It was wonderful how words like *ghosts and curses* could be absolutely wiped out by words like *smashing girl*.

·IV·

"No," decreed Mrs. Berry, the little dictator, "you don't want to look like a widow."

Without a word Lucia returned the conservative dark dress to her wardrobe and took out a garnet-red silk suit, still fairly conservative but a more interesting foil for her hair. It was Friday morning, and Mrs. Berry had decided she'd better see to Lucia's dress for the party in case it needed pressing, which meant, as Lucia knew perfectly well, in order to pass judgment on it. And how she knew Lucia *wasn't* a widow, Lucia didn't question. Mr. Slade, Mr. Farr's estate agent, may have told her, but Lucia supposed it was one of those things women found out about each other instinctively, without being told.

"Aye, that will do," pronounced Mrs. Berry.

"I'm glad it meets with your approval."

"Aye," she said, ignoring Lucia's irony, "the red is more congenial." She took the suit from Lucia's hand and trotted away with it.

But she had uttered the right word.

Lucia had believed there were those who shone at cocktail parties, like Julian, and those who did not, like herself, and being guest of honor in strange company in a strange land only increased her mounting stage fright. How would she manage, deprived of the consoling shadow cast by Julian's sun and utterly on her own?

Now Mrs. Berry without knowing it had told her how. It wasn't necessary to shine. It wasn't necessary to be a wit, or a beauty, or a celebrity. It was necessary only to be congenial.

Nevertheless Lucia took pains with her appearance that evening, applying her most subtle makeup, a porcelain finish that hid freckles, followed by a delicate blush, eye shadow, mascara, and a final touch of luster on her lips. Her hair shone like freshly polished copper. She wore pumps that matched her suit and pearls over a cream satin blouse, and when she stood fully dressed before the long mirror in the front bedroom, her reflection—although she wouldn't herself use the word *smashing*—brought out a glow that co-ordinated the ensemble.

No one this evening would have called her stony-faced.

It had grown steadily warmer throughout the week, and today Lucia had heard voices on the Admiral's side of her garden wall indicating he planned to entertain out of doors. But it had also grown steadily cloudier and moister, and as Lucia set out from her front steps to the Admiral's front steps, she saw an ominous darkening beyond St. Wilfred's tower and hoped whatever was gathering there was far enough away to hold off at least for a couple of hours.

THE Admiral opened the door to her. She was so much

more attractive than he remembered that his great eyebrows shot up over a stare. Then instantly recovering himself he drew her indoors, wheeled about smartly, offering her his arm, and conducted her like royalty through his trim house to his trim garden. A few people were already gathered there, and he fetched her a drink and introduced her punctiliously, although as more people arrived she gave up hope of keeping their names straight.

"Never mind," said Peg Goodfriend, wearing a serviceable polyester print. The Reverend Goodfriend careened and wobbled from guest to guest, but Peg planted herself on a single spot on the grass and stayed there, holding her glass without fidgeting. "You'll get us sorted out in time. It's so much easier for a lot of people to meet one person than for one person to meet a lot of people."

And Lucia, laughing, warmed to her for that.

Iris Goodfriend stepped up to offer Lucia her hand and show her fetching dimple. Tonight she wore khaki jodhpurs, red leg warmers over riding boots, and a black sequin top; her hair was again done in spikes and she wore red eye shadow. It was hard not to voice the thought uppermost in one's mind, such as, "What a sensational outfit," but Lucia bravely looked away and said everyone in Foxwold must be there, to which Iris answered, "God."

Underneath it all, Lucia could see, Iris was a pretty girl. Perhaps when she ran out of outlandish things to do to her hair and jumble-sale things to wear, to say nothing of broadening her vocabulary, she would more nearly resemble a product of a centuries-old civilization. Or perhaps the evidence of civilization lay in the fact that no one at the party gave her a second glance. Tolerance for eccentricity, Lucia was learning here in England, was an attribute of mellowed humanity.

The garden was soon filled with people, and the Admiral was plainly on the bridge: aware, responsible, gallant, ironhanded. Again and again he materialized at Lucia's elbow to rescue her from a longwinded oldster or to present another guest. "*So-o-o-o* happy to meet you!" women caroled in a descending full-octave glissando, from B-flat to C-sharp, and chatted on agreeably about the weather, America, writing books, and so on.

"D'you ride?" a Mrs. O'Bailey wanted to know, straight off, with an unequivocal stare.

"Ride?" Lucia reiterated witlessly, but at once she realized the muscular woman, too weather-beaten for her blue chiffon, would look extremely handsome in black hunting coat with tan collar, and she answered, "No, I'm afraid not."

"Golf?"

"No."

"Tennis?"

"No."

"Good lord, what *do* you do?"

"I walk."

"Oh." Mrs. O'Bailey uttered the monosyllable not with disdain so much as pity. She was saddened by Lucia as some people are depressed by the retarded or handicapped.

The Admiral bore Mrs. O'Bailey away, replacing her with the Winters, a nice young couple who lived at the far end of Church Street next to the rectory. Lucia and the Winters were having a pleasant chat when the Ambrose sisters arrived, escorted by their fair-haired great-nephew. The sisters were waylaid by friends immediately, but the nephew searched the company until he located Lucia, and then made a bee-line across the grass to her.

"Hello, Lucia Vail," he said happily and the Winters, aware that he was interested only in Lucia, eased themselves away. "I'm Simon Myles. That glimpse of you in your doorway didn't half do you justice."

He had deep blue eyes with creases of merriment fanning out from the corners. He was the kind of young man, Lucia guessed, who was facetious when he was serious, and serious when he was facetious. His thick blond hair was brushed across the top of his head and back over his ears in the English gentleman's style, but it rebelled and curled up at the edges, giving him a schoolboyish look for all his elegant clothes.

"Was it destiny, or incredible luck," he prattled on, "that brought you all the way from the States to Church Street, Foxwold, North Yorkshire, next door to my favorite aunts?"

"It was my editor," she told him, deciding upon candor as the best way to play his ingenuous game. People were apt to be wary of writers and he might as well know the worst right off. "He recommended Foxwold because I'm working on a novel about Charlotte Brontë." Not to mention a badly damaged ego.

"Yes," said Simon, unfazed, "my aunts told me you're an author." It was always nicer to be called an author than a writer, and Lucia felt herself unbending. "I've pumped them shamelessly," he told her, "for information about you. You've been to the parsonage at Haworth, of course?"

"No, I've been saving it until I got settled here."

"Oh, then," he bent toward her eagerly, "look, Lucia Vail: Would you consider it too forward of me—good God, I'm *talking* like a Brontë—would you let me drive you there? Would you let me take you to Haworth for the first time?"

It was the farthest thing from her mind, to visit Haworth with someone else, least of all with a fast-talking stranger. It was to be a pilgrimage, too important, too emotional, to undertake until all extraneous concerns such as finding a house and getting moved in, even the foolish anxiety over a cocktail party, were behind her.

"Certainly," she said. Because she liked the creases of merriment beside the deep blue eyes. Because making a pilgrimage alone suddenly didn't seem the most exalted way of doing it. "I'd love it."

34

"Oh, marvelous. We'll go next week, shall we? Will you be settled by then? I'll ring you."

"Yes, all right."

The aunts were advancing, burbling and hallooing and leaving behind them a convivial wake. "There now," cried Adelaide, "you've found her, Simon, and she's just as nice as you thought, isn't she?"

"Nice," he replied, with his look of combined gaiety and gravity, "is hardly the word. She is much nicer than nice."

Gentle Olivia touched Lucia's hand. "Don't let them embarrass you, dear. Between them they can be quite naughty."

"In any case," cried Adelaide, "here comes Willie to shoo us along. He's had his eye on you, Simon. Mustn't monopolize the guest of honor. Royal Navy to the rescue, eh, Willie? Full steam ahead!"

"We live next door to her, old trout." No one but Adelaide called the Admiral Willie, and no one but the Admiral called Adelaide old trout. "Others are less fortunate."

"Far less," agreed Simon.

"Goodbye then, Lucia; you look lovely!"

"You do, dear," echoed Olivia.

Simon bent over Lucia's hand, not quite touching it with his lips. "Until next week," he murmured, and then he linked arms with his aunts and wheeled them away.

The light had been fading into a greenish gloom. There was now a slight, preliminary rumble of thunder in the west, but the party guests, after a skyward glance, went on making their genteel hubbub.

"Here's Dr. Jenna," said the Admiral. "Glad you could come, dear chap. You've met Mrs. Vail? I'll leave you to make her acquaintance." And Dr. Jenna had no choice but to give her his hand, thin and dry, light and remote.

Lucia found it hard to imagine such a hand voluntarily touching diseased flesh, or even healthy flesh; but perhaps the sick found his touch soothing.

"Did you hear the thunder?" he asked.

"Yes. Do you think it will rain?"

"Perhaps. One cannot predict with accuracy. The sound of thunder may not be as ominous as it seems."

She felt all at once as if they were talking in parables. Perhaps it was this odd, rather mystical slant to their conversation that prompted her to say, "I thought I heard another ominous sound in the night recently. A cry of sadness."

"Indeed?" He had kept his finely chiseled profile turned from her, but now he faced about and his heavy dark eyes came to rest on hers. "How interesting," he said softly, encouraging her to continue.

"I thought it might be an owl."

"Do you sleep in the front bedroom?"

"No," she replied, startled, "in the back." What had the bedroom to do with it?

"And did the cry come from the garden?"

"No, from the front. I thought from the street."

"Ah." The heavy eyes, purplish in the twilight, turned away again (was there a tiny flicker of cognizance before they turned?). "Perhaps an owl, perhaps not." He cast his glance over the crowded garden as though planning his way out when the polite moment came to escape. "Have you heard it again since then?"

"No." He *was* mysterious, as Adelaide had said. Lucia wondered if he smoked an exotic hallucinatory herb of the East or went into self-hypnotic trances. It was partly a buoyant mood left over from her meeting with Simon and partly a challenging desire to penetrate Dr. Jenna's remoteness that made her say, "I'm beginning to think there's something about Bloodrose House that everyone knows and no one wants to tell me."

"It is possible," he answered, to her surprise. He faced her once more, the purplish eyes wandering impersonally over her. "But it has nothing to do with you. You are young and beautiful, an enemy of old sorrows. Be at peace. Enjoy life."

And like a priest after uttering a benediction, Dr. Jenna moved on. The Admiral was returning.

"Are you warm enough?" inquired Luddington. "Shall we go inside?"

Another gust, this time creating a great sigh among the trees, passed overhead, and Lucia and the Admiral and nearly everyone else paused in mid-sentence. Only one voice, vaguely and unpleasantly familiar, went on talking.

In the rapidly increasing twilight, Lucia made out the figure of a man, his back turned and stooped slightly as he conversed with someone shorter than himself, and there was no mistaking the incisive voice with its trace of arrogance. It was the farmer who had ordered her off his land.

At the same moment there was a full-fledged rumble of thunder, almost overhead, and the first heavy drops of rain were flung out at random on the wind.

The Admiral took Lucia's elbow, and everyone began to rush, laughing and hooting, toward the door into the house. Inside there was further confusion as people milled about, debating whether to stay or leave, and Lucia decided to make a dash for home.

The Admiral wished to escort her to her door, but a firm hand reached for the umbrella and the imperious voice said, "Let me, Will. See to your guests," an order which, apparently, even the Admiral must obey.

Lucia had taken in little but the ruddy coloring of the farmer's face last week, but now, close to, in the Admiral's well-lighted hall, the face turned out to be long and black-browed, with a long nose and claret-colored stains, like blush marks, down the cheeks. The brows were worn in a frown and the dark eyes edgy.

He said, with a faint twist of a grin that didn't erase the

frown, "So you are my tenant, Mrs. Vail," and she realized the rude farmer, her landlord, and the Honourable Antony Farr were all one.

"Yes," she responded crisply, "and I'm perfectly able to run next door by myself, if you'll let me borrow the umbrella."

"No," he said, a man obviously used to having his own way, "I'll take you."

It wasn't worth arguing about, and having thanked Will Luddington and said good night, she let Antony Farr guide her down one walk and up the other in the pelting rain.

But under her front-door light, while he held the umbrella over their heads and she delved into her purse for her key, he said without preamble, "It was unpardonable, warning you so peremptorily off Farthing land. I thought you were just another blundering American tourist."

That didn't improve matters. "Well, and so I was," she answered shortly. Perhaps the deep dogmatic voice would rub her the wrong way no matter what he said. The rain thumped on the black silk umbrella. "And I'd rather be blundering than boorish."

"I almost came back to apologize," he told her, brows scowling, knuckles white on the umbrella handle. "Too bloody proud."

"Okay, forget it," she said, laying on the American off-handedness. "We're getting wet. Will you come in?"

"No!" he cried sharply, as if recoiling.

The invitation was a token courtesy, so mechanical that it had come out involuntarily, not meant to be accepted, but she didn't expect quite so vehement a refusal.

He sucked in his breath and let it out; it was exasperating, the sigh implied, trying to right a wrong and only making things worse. "I'm sorry for my rudeness to you," he finished more evenly, as if he must have the last word, "and I do apologize most sincerely, and there, that is that. I've said it and I mean it. Good night."

And he stalked off into the rain, tall, hunched over, in an indefinable way more elegant than Simon Myles but in no way as agreeable; highstrung, irritable, and solitary. He turned up the Admiral's steps and disappeared into Will's house.

Lucia went inside and closed her door.

Across the street, the lighted chink between the curtains closed also.

·V·

A SPELL of chilly weather settled in, in the wake of the thunder storm, and a wet wind swept down off Ravensmoor, looming up darkly beyond and behind Bloodrose House. The central heating tempered the chill but didn't really warm the house, at least not by American standards, and Lucia was more than ever grateful for her coal fire and snug study.

Simon telephoned Saturday.

"You haven't changed your mind?" he said at once. "You will go to Haworth with me? Or rather, let me go to Haworth with you? I can just manage to wait until Tuesday. Would Tuesday suit you?"

"Tuesday would be fine, but if it's raining like this—"

"It may well be. In Britain you must learn not to let rain interfere with anything. Besides, you should see Haworth in the rain, you won't know Charlotte Brontë completely until you do. I'll come for you about eleven and we'll lunch at Betty's in Harrogate. There are grander places, but Betty's is an institution. Lucia, I look forward exceedingly to Tuesday!"

They hung up.

It was a relief not to be forced to take charge and then feel guilty about it. It had been Lucia's unlucky experience that charm in a man went hand-in-hand with a tendency towards helplessness. Simon Myles, despite his light touch, gave evidence of being competent, well-organized, and reliable. Yet not arrogant or domineering.

On Sunday it rained again, but Lucia, wearing a tweed suit and wool pullover, raincoat with wool liner, rain hat and rubber boots, forced herself out of the house, and walked up to St. Wilfred's for the 9:30 service, a Sung Eucharist with Sermon, as described in gilt letters on a notice board.

Founded by Saxons in the eighth century, St. Wilfred's had been summarily torn down and rebuilt by Normans after the Conquest, converted to the Perpendicular style in the late fourteenth century, and further embellished, though not fatally, by Tudors, Elizabethans, Jacobeans, Georgians, and Victorians. It was noted for its melodious bells, each of which had a Latin inscription and its own affectionate nickname.

This morning the altar and the window sills were bright with scarlet tulips, but the Edwardian stoves were even less effective than Lucia's central heating, and breath rose from the pews in plumes. The Reverend Goodfriend, however, officiated stirringly, with a rare combination of dispatch and dignity, his versatile voice singing out the ancient chants and encouraging the congregation to rouse themselves and respond without timidity. His sermon was brisk, the underlying message being: God *is,* and you had better cooperate with Him fully.

In an atmosphere of such vigorous devotion, in a building so old and so infused with the selfless and spiritual, bodily comfort was inconsequential.

But afterwards on the way out, with the prospect of a rainy Sunday afternoon far from home, far from friends, far even from the Sunday *New York Times,* far indeed from Julian, Lucia paused on the spur of the moment near the door to issue an invitation to tea to Peg and Iris Goodfriend, who were collecting prayer books and replacing them in the racks from which they had initially handed them out.

"Delighted!" exclaimed Peg, but Iris, who was wearing what looked like a medium-sized Oriental rug, said she was sorry, she had a date, and actually sounded sorry. Cedric Goodfriend, shaking hands under the dripping porch, accepted provided he could slip away early to a committee meeting. The Admiral came out just then, and Lucia invited him too.

Sunday gloom dispelled, she hurried home to bake an almond cake, one of her specialties, and assemble tea things.

She used the sitting room for the first time. At four o'clock she drew the heavy curtains against the darkening day, turned on lamps, and lighted the log fire, with the result that Mrs. Berry's brilliantly polished brass and shining china sparkled all the more, and the room with its riotous roses was as cheerful as could be.

"Well, well, well," said Peg, plumping herself down on one of the small sofas and gazing about her. "Lady Quelling-Steele really went all out, didn't she?"

"It looks like her," pronounced her husband cryptically, as he folded his gawky frame onto a Victorian chair.

Peg interpolated for Lucia: "Terribly chic but a bit overpowering. Her Jaguar is upholstered in leopardskin, need I say more?"

"No. I've met her; she dropped in last week. *Real* leopardskin?"

"I don't dare ask. But real or not the implication is clear: Female Carnivore."

Lucia, pouring tea, glanced at Peg with new respect. There were no blinders on her eyes, and only a very slight bridle on her tongue.

"Still, this is an improvement," moderated Cedric charitably. "The old decor, if you could call it that, was rather dark."

"It was," agreed Peg. "Helen never liked Bloodrose House or put much into it."

Lucia looked from one to the other, guessing Helen was a previous tenant, but not understanding why the Goodfriends were now curiously silent, as though containing thoughts best not expressed.

A smart rap of the front door knocker sounded and Lucia went to admit the Admiral. When he had joined the circle they commenced a pleasant hashing-over of his party. Old friends were tallied and bits of information exchanged, while Lucia, listening quietly, replenished cups and cake plates. The fire burned brightly; the rain pattered on the window panes.

"Wasn't it nice that Tony came?" The Admiral gave Lucia a deferential nod. "In honor of his new tenant, of course."

"He would come because you asked him, Will," pointed out Cedric, "though I don't mean to minimize Lucia's drawing power."

"Oh, one never knows with Tony," protested Will, with a modest nose-whistle. "He hasn't become antisocial exactly, but he's not gregarious either. Ever since—well, there it is."

Again Lucia searched their faces. Ever since what?

"I'm surprised he still lets the Festival use Farthing for concerts," said Peg, "and holds the Harvest Ball in October. Public-spiritedness, no doubt. He's never let down in *that* area."

"Might they not be memorials?" suggested Cedric. "Helen started them both."

Helen again. Helen who?

"In any case, Farthing's not *his* house," continued Cedric, "it's his brother's, and though George was never known for public-spiritedness, he may like keeping up the old lord-of-the-manor traditions, even by remote control."

Lucia was now entirely at sea.

"I doubt that George knows or cares *what* goes on at Farthing," said Peg. "I hear he's not in the best of health."

"Too much brandy and cigars!" barked Will, whistling disapproval. "To say nothing of mademoiselles. Bound to take its toll at his age. Don't mean to be disrespectful, but since he never bothers with Farthing, indeed has all but turned his back on English soil, he leaves himself open to criticism."

Someone at last took notice of Lucia's bewilderment. "Sorry, my dear," said Peg. "We're speaking of Lord Ravensmoor, who lives in the south of France."

"Mr. Farr's brother?"

Peg nodded.

"Older, of course," said the Admiral. "Too bad. Tony should have inherited Farthing. Lives there alone now. Loves it, works hard to keep it going. Best farmer in the countryside. Quite unfair."

The conversation branched off into a general review of the ancient rites of succession, and Lucia had no chance to ask any more questions.

Cedric Goodfriend looked at his watch and sprang to his feet. "Speaking of the Festival, I must run. There's a meeting of the committee at five." The Foxwold Festival, late in June, a week of concerts, organ recitals, and Morris dancing in the square, was already being advertised in the village. "Thank you, Lucia, for that celestial cake." He touched Peg's knee in passing. "See you after evensong."

Lucia accompanied him out to the hall, where with a flurry of flying sleeves and belts he got into his raincoat and scurried away.

Will departed soon after. Bertie must have his walk, rain or shine. He had left Bertie at home because, he explained, in wet weather he was inclined to stink.

"What a very nice man," said Lucia, returning to her place opposite Peg.

"They don't come any nicer," agreed Peg.

"He must have had an illustrious career in the Navy."

There was another of those little restrained silences, almost too brief to notice, and then Peg said, "One might think so."

It was a highly ambiguous reply, and Lucia looked up sharply. "You mean—he didn't?"

Peg studied her teacup. "You may as well hear it from me as from someone else. He's not an admiral."

"He's *not?*"

"It all came out two or three years ago. Mind you, he never actually *said* he was an Admiral; he simply acted the part so well that everyone assumed he was, and he let them. When anyone asked him about his part in the war he put up his hands and begged off with, 'That's ancient history,' or words to that effect, which one took for modesty. When it came out that he'd served as a junior officer in a minor desk job, he almost died of shame. It was all over town, of course. We feared he might do something really drastic. It was Cedric who persuaded him to carry on. After all, he'd never lied, he'd never falsified documents, he'd never put on a false uniform. And so, bless him, he braved the world and held up his head again, and I do believe we loved him the more for it. So if you catch a wink or a nudge from someone, that's what it means. Now, I'd better tear myself away, too." Peg got to her feet. "Iris will be bringing her ravenous cycling friends home for fodder."

"Would you like to see the rest of the house before you go?"

"Love to! I'm dying to see it."

They went over the downstairs first, sharing breezy comments, and then went upstairs, finishing with the front bedroom.

There, in the door, Peg stood in silence for what seemed a long time.

Why was this room important, a kind of reference point,

44

to the people of Foxwold? Lucia held her tongue, hoping Peg would throw some light on the matter.

"A bit tarty, isn't it?" said Peg at last, and she turned to Lucia with a faint smile. "I've no doubt that Lady Quelling-Steele hoped to make use of it herself."

"What, you mean she wanted to live here?"

"I mean," said Peg, "she had rather a fancy for Tony Farr. My daughter would say at this point, '*God*, mother,' and she's right, I'm far too outspoken for a vicar's wife. My husband, a better Christian, is more circumlocutory."

"Peg, I don't believe circumlocution is more Christian than outspokenness. I admire anyone who can even *say* circumlocutory."

Peg's dry smile warmed to a grin. "Lucia, you gladden my heart. Now I must go. But look here, if you should tire of your typewriter and wish to go sightseeing or shopping or simply want company, ring me, I'd love to assist."

They went downstairs where Peg deftly put on her raincoat, not forgetting anything, gave Lucia a squeeze of the hand, and took herself off without another unnecessary word.

It was good for a damaged ego when an attractive man called one smashing, Lucia acknowledged as she washed up the tea things, but what she felt this evening was more comforting than ego-gratification, a tranquil emotion one seldom had room for in New York: simple, uncluttered, unfettered fondness. She had become very fond of Peg and Cedric Goodfriend, of Will Luddington the would-be Admiral, of Adelaide and Olivia Ambrose, and she sensed it was the answer to the displacement syndrome, that sense of being far from home, far from Julian.

Fondness made a rainy day seem cozy, and not working seem not wasteful, and being alone not lonely.

Of Peg Goodfriend she thought, *There* is someone who might level with me, although Lucia wasn't quite sure at the moment what she would ask Peg to level with her about. *Tell me about Bloodrose House* might do for starters, but it might not lead where she wanted it to lead.

And where she wanted it to lead she didn't know either. Her awareness of something unexplained had begun to hover over her like a gathering cloud.

·VI·

THE wet spell broke up on Tuesday with a strong breeze and low scudding clouds. Sunlight pure as spring water flowered into bloom every few minutes and closed again.

Lucia was dressing for her pilgrimage to Haworth when there was a loud banging of the front door knocker, and soon Mrs. Berry came upstairs to say Miss Adelaide wanted a word with her. Lucia, buttoning her blouse, went down at once, and Mrs. Berry retired to the kitchen.

"Sorry, Lucia, I shan't keep you!" Adelaide waited inside the door. "Just wanted to invite you to lunch Sunday, I do hope you're free!"

"Yes, how nice, Adelaide, I'd love to come."

"Good. One o'clock. Glad I caught you. Simon told us you're stopping in Harrogate. I'm happy the weather's improving; the gardens should be lovely." Adelaide's small bright intelligent eyes sought Lucia's face. "He is a dear, isn't he? How I *wish* he'd settle down!"

At once Lucia's smile became slightly fixed. Was Adelaide hinting Simon needed a mate? Or was she, Lucia, being warned not to trifle with a favorite nephew's affections?

Whatever Adelaide had in mind, Lucia guessed it was the real purpose of her call.

"Surely he will someday," replied Lucia noncommittally.

Adelaide opened the front door and stepped out into the breeze. "He gives no sign of doing so," she said with a sigh.

A terrible thought struck Lucia. "Adelaide, you don't mean he's—he's—" How to imply *gay* to an eighty-five-year-old retired English schoolteacher? *Homosexual* seemed too clinical, and *effeminate* too delicate—

"*Queer?*" shrieked Adelaide, heedless of the open doors and windows up and down the street, and she gave a shout of laughter. "No, my dear, no!" Tears of mirth filled her eyes.

"But he just doesn't fall in love?" persisted Lucia.

Adelaide seemed in a fair way to collapse on the doorstep. She crooked an elbow and, convulsed, leaned against the jamb.

"He falls in love," she was able to gasp at last, "at the drop of a hat. That's what I'm trying to tell you! A darling he is, so thoughtful of his aunties, of everyone who crosses his path, but he falls in love *all the time*." She straightened. "I've said enough. I mustn't keep you. I'm off to round up bachelors for Sunday. I'll count on Simon for one, if you've no objection. Enjoy your outing!"

And cape flying, Adelaide made her way back to her house next door.

Adelaide wasn't trying to protect Simon from Lucia, thought Lucia, smiling, as she closed the door; but rather Lucia from Simon.

ODDLY, Adelaide's warning had a relaxing effect. It eliminated guesswork and skirmishing. No pitfalls lay ahead now. A man who fell in love at the drop of a hat was in his way as harmless as a man who wasn't interested in women at all. When Simon Myles arrived at her door half an hour later, she greeted him with a friendly, unreserved, open-and-aboveboard smile.

They headed south in the white Mercedes. Simon avoided the A1 motorway with its thundering lorries and took the old winding roads through farmland, rolling and jewel-green, sometimes freshly plowed and russet, here and there a vivid yellow. When Lucia asked Simon what the yellow stuff was, he told her, with a roll of the r, "rape." To which Lucia gave a slow, uncomprehending, nothing–surprises–me New York shrug, which made Simon laugh. The wind blew, diligently sweeping April out of the way to make way for May, and the sun continually burst out from behind low-flying clouds. Washing flapped on clotheslines; tractors with their glassed–in drivers' seats traversed the fields. Everyone was astir this bright, brisk morning after the rain.

Prompting her with droll half-questions and listening attentively to her answers, Simon made it his business as they rolled along to find out all about her. "Something tells me you were an only child, am I right? A certain quietness, as if you were used to being rather solitary."

His intuitions were highly tuned and she was buoyed again into the carefree mood he cultivated at a cocktail party or over the telephone. There was nothing like being listened to attentively. Inside of an hour, Simon Myles knew more about her than Julian had ever known or cared to know.

"But with the Saxon name of Fairburn, how did you come by the Latin one of Lucia? Even though you pronounce it the English way, to rhyme with fuchsia?"

She told him about an admired grandmother with the name of Lucy, which Lucia's parents altered slightly as befitting a baby with red hair. "If you follow me," said Lucia.

"Of course." He nodded solemnly. "Lucia sounds much more red-headed than Lucy."

Soon, thought Lucia with misgivings, he would ask her about her marriage. But his instincts were more sure-footed than that. He didn't refer to it at all.

They entered Harrogate in a flood of sunlight which seemed to promise the sky had been swept clean at last. At

Simon's suggestion they parked the car and walked down the length of a long open park under great old trees and their lacy foliage, past formal gardens and ornate Victorian hotels, and finally to Betty's on the edge of the shopping district.

The cheerful sprawling restaurant was filled with late coffee-drinkers and early lunchers, but Simon with a knack of getting what he wanted without fuss, contrived to secure a table in a sunlit window overlooking the gardens. They sat down opposite each other and ordered coffee, and next, having recommended the Dover sole, he carefully ordered lunch with a dry white wine.

The English, remarked Lucia, eyeing the brilliant scene outside the window, did surprising things with flowers. "Pink and white tulips mixed with orange and white wallflowers! Bordered by yellow pansies! Purple tulips in a bed of blue forget-me-nots! It's positively wanton."

"Reserved people have to break out somehow," replied Simon.

She turned to him. "How do you break out, Simon, dare I ask?"

"I don't have to. I'm an open book to begin with."

"Anyone who claims he's an open book usually isn't."

"Try me."

"All right, let's hear about *your* childhood."

He told her about a boy with two bossy sisters growing up in a fairly unsupervised way in a boarding school where his father was an overworked and underpaid headmaster. "I was a brat—conniving, sadistic, and fat. The only adult who had any influence over me was my great-aunt Adelaide, to whom I was sent for the holidays, and I loved her for it. It was she who got me interested in collecting things, and from butterflies and stamps I graduated to paperweights and snuff boxes, and at last I applied myself to a book or two and eventually my talents, such as they are, found fulfillment in the antiques trade."

She smiled, certain he hadn't painted a true picture of

himself. She appraised the deep-blue, crease-cornered eyes, the irrepressible blond hair, the figure in the beautifully cut twill which while not thin was by no means fat, and she thought in all likelihood he must have been a very appealing lad.

And how susceptible was *she*, she quite unexpectedly asked herself, to falling in love with *him?*

He was looking straight into her eyes, smiling back at her as if he could read her thoughts.

She pulled herself up short, rubbed the bridge of her nose, and applied herself to the Dover sole. "Your mother?" she asked hurriedly. It was the first thing that came to mind, perhaps because his mother was the one relative he hadn't mentioned. "Could she do nothing with you?"

"Probably not. She died when I was three. I remember very little about her." (And did this account for his infatuations, conjectured Lucia?) "What a dull story," he said, putting an end to it. "I'd so much rather fathom those metamorphic eyes of yours. Are they green, or gray, or brown, or all three?"

She shook her head. "You're incorrigible, Simon, even if your Aunt Adelaide didn't think so."

"Would that it were true. What my Aunt Adelaide discerned, and what endures, I fear, is a latent, low-level, fatal corrigibility, which crops out now and then and leads me to commit unmitigated decencies." He raised his glass. "To this delightful moment, Lucia Vail."

At ease and enjoying themselves, they drank.

When they came out of the restaurant the fickle spring weather had changed; the clouds had come up again and a raw wind blew down from the north.

Simon slipped an arm companionably through Lucia's.

"To Haworth," he said, in such a way that she caught her breath in a little gulp of emotion. And from then on Simon was thoughtfully subdued, saying scarcely a word as they drove farther south, leaving her to her feelings.

They turned off the main road at last at Keighley, where government signs directed them to Haworth and the Brontë Museum.

This, thought Lucia, was the last mile. Along this road, returning with heavy heart from Brussels or London, often in the rain and driven by more piercing winds, passing these self-same blackened houses, walked Charlotte Brontë.

They entered the town, but there was still another climb to the parsonage. Simon left the car in one of the several public car parks, and they followed the signs up the street.

Already Lucia realized how ludicrous her dream of a private pilgrimage was. The Brontës belonged to the world and this was an international shrine. Even in April the car parks were occupied. The rugged young couple in shorts climbing the hill ahead of them conversed in French. A party of Japanese, festooned with cameras, passed on their way down.

Charlotte wouldn't have believed it.

But Lucia now trod literally in Charlotte's footsteps as well as spiritually. The cobblestones under the lowering sky, the stone of the somber houses, even those rigged out to sell Brontë souvenirs, were all of a grayness to chill the soul, and as Simon had predicted, in the grayness she saw the more stringently Charlotte's despair and fortitude.

One by one the brother and sisters for whom she'd borne such tenderness had dropped away, first Maria and Elizabeth, then hapless Branwell and difficult Emily, and finally most beloved Anne, and then Charlotte was alone. Their father kept to his parlor with the door shut. What a house to come home to!

There still was the Black Bull, the pub where Branwell found escape and drank his short life away, and there now was Haworth Old Church, gray also and austere in its wilderness of blackened tombs, familiar from the photograph made in Charlotte's day. (The photograph included a tiny female figure, considered by many to be Charlotte herself, taking the air outside the parsonage.) And now they were turning into a lane, the final yards of Charlotte's long desolate walk, and there at last, tall and gray-black, stood the parsonage itself.

Lucia came to a halt, vaguely aware of other pilgrims milling about her (if it was this crowded in April, what was it like in July?), but she had all but transferred herself to the nineteenth century. From that famous photograph she knew no shrubbery had softened the angles of the bare house as it did now, no trees screened the bleak sky, probably no yellow tulips grew against the bare stone, and Lucia envisioned the house without them.

Tears flooded up behind her eyes, pulled at her throat. She too, in a sense, had come home.

Considerately Simon beside her let her work it out, and presently, with one or two quick gulps, she got hold of herself. She felt Simon's light touch under her elbow, and they went in.

On the left was the dining room where brother and sisters created their tiny fantasy books, where they must in those early days have shared laughter. But there on that uncomfortable-looking horsehair sofa Emily had died.

Across the hall was Patrick's brooding place, and on the table were his pipe and Bible and spectacles just as he had left them, outliving all his children, at the age of eighty-four.

And this was the kitchen where shy Emily, helping Tabbie their faithful servant, felt safe from the world.

But it was upstairs that Charlotte most movingly came alive. Here was her plain brown dress, perhaps the very one she had worn to London and had no choice but to wear to the opera with her friends the Smiths, a dress that would scarcely fit a present-day child of nine. Here were her tiny gloves and slippers, a bracelet, a ring containing a lock of Anne's blonde hair. Here were Emily's death certificate (consumption) and Charlotte's (phthisis).

Again Lucia had to grapple with a swell of emotion.

They finished the afternoon in the museum behind the parsonage, and privately Lucia promised herself to return soon and go over it all again more carefully.

Simon took a shortcut on the way back, over Rombolds Moor, and on a deserted heather-dark height he stopped the car, dried with a clean handkerchief the tears that had at last spilled out on Lucia's cheek, considered her face for a moment, then took her in his arms and kissed her on the lips, softly and lingeringly. And all at once Lucia wanted to kiss him passionately back, surrender to him entirely. At the same time, her brain told her this overwrought response had little to do with Simon or even with her own prolonged celibacy, but a lot to do with Charlotte and the terrible, unreasonable tragedies of life.

Gently Lucia drew back, out of Simon's arms, and he let her go without a struggle, reading her mind again perhaps, although he took a minute to look out the window on his side of the car and calm down. "Charlotte married in the end, didn't she?" he asked as though nothing had happened. "She had a few months of happiness before the onset of this—phthisis, whatever that is."

"It means wasting away. She was pregnant. The nausea killed her. She was a frail thing to begin with."

He made a sound of dismay. "So much for wedded bliss!"

"It could be controlled easily today. But you're right, Simon. It's not fair to make a tragedy of her life. She not only had a few months of happiness with her Mr. Nicholls, she had recognition and honors in her own time. People made pilgrimages to her even then." Lucia opened her purse and repaired her disheveled face and hair. She looked brighter; Simon's kiss may have been restorative after all. "Her life was not a tragedy, really, but a triumph."

"And you will write a triumphant book, I haven't the slightest doubt." He started the engine again. "We'll stop for tea somewhere and then I thought we might go on to

York. I'd love you to see my digs, and there's quite a decent place to have dinner . . ."

"Tea," she said, "by all means." Like many Americans in Britain she was almost more addicted to afternoon tea than the British. "But, Simon, it's been a very affecting day. I'd be poor company at dinner." She wanted time to assimilate all she'd taken in, and she wasn't up to handling the possibilities of being alone with Simon in his digs. "I'd really like to go home."

"All right. I won't press you. You are rather spent, aren't you? I'll take you home after tea and have dinner with my aunts next door."

Suddenly a way seemed to open, and she took it, not quite knowing where it would lead. "Have your aunts always lived next door to Bloodrose House?"

"Ever since I can remember. They bought their house when their father left them a little money."

"And you've been visiting them since childhood. Tell me, Simon, *does* Bloodrose House—I mean, *is* it supposed to have a ghost?"

"Good God, I hope not!"

"You've never heard of its having one?"

He considered. "Now that you mention it, I think while it was unoccupied some of the villagers tried to invent one."

"Why?" she persisted. "What went on there? Why do people hint at something and then quickly change the subject?"

He turned to give her a quick grin. They were rolling over the dark moor again. "What went on there was no different from what goes on in all houses: love, death, and so on." Was he really as unconcerned as he sounded? "Not as dramatic as the Brontë parsonage, perhaps, but distinguished by the fact that in Foxwold the Ravensmoor family are VIPs."

"And who was Helen?"

There was a split second before he answered, a tiny shift

54

of subjective tone barely perceptible except to a listener acutely tuned to nuances, as if her question had finally shaken his nonchalance. His voice dropped slightly. "Helen was Tony Farr's wife."

"Was? Where is she now?"

"She is in her grave."

The skin on Lucia's arm shrank in gooseflesh. Why hadn't he simply said dead? "How did she die?"

"She had cancer."

Recklessly then, but prompted by an odd note in his voice, she asked, "Did you like her?"

"I wouldn't say liked her," he replied, lightly but rather distantly, as if it were time Lucia left off. "She was something of a saint, you know."

A saint? For some reason Lucia found this quite unexpected. Perhaps it was the hint of cynicism in his voice. She matched her voice to his. "Saints aren't likable?"

He reached for her wrist and pressed it in a silencing way. "Enough of graves!" He gave her another grin. "Life goes on! We drank to the present, remember? See, we're coming into Otley. I think I know where we can get tea by a hearth fire." He slowed the car as they entered the high street.

"From this moment on," he said, watching for the place he had in mind, "until we must part, let us talk about ourselves and look on the brighter side of things." He applied the brakes and drew up before an inn. "This is where we stop for tea."

He, too, had changed the subject.

· *VII* ·

APRIL merged into May. Hawthorn and crab apple burst into bloom. The thick red branches clinging to the walls of Bloodrose House began to put forth leaf buds, tightly furled and sharp as their own thorns. In the distance the great brown whale-back of Ravensmoor took on a subtle hint of green.

Lucia did go back to Haworth, and her work underwent an even more favorable change. She began a second draft incorporating a greater understanding and assurance, and her principal characters seemed to step fully rounded out of the page.

One afternoon at work she pulled open the center drawer of her desk without looking, reaching blindly for an eraser, and felt the heavy molding along the bottom of the drawer give way. Dismayed, she thought she'd broken something on the beautiful old desk, but looking down she found the molding was on hinges and had dropped open, revealing a shallow compartment, or false bottom.

A secret drawer! Perhaps it held some treasure, a packet of eighteenth-century love letters . . .

But it held nothing but a few bills, dating back only a few years, held together with a paper clip. *For Services Rendered,* £378.40. *For Services Rendered,* £853.78. And so on. They were all headed Ellerbee & Son, 22 South Gate, York, and they were all addressed to the Hon. Mrs. Antony Farr.

A garage? A furniture store?

Lucia, losing interest, returned them to the drawer and

snapped the molding shut. Some of the bills had been marked paid and presumably the rest had been settled also; there was no need to bring them to anyone's attention. They had been tucked in the back of the drawer and must have been overlooked when the desk was cleaned out.

For a long time, Lucia didn't give them another thought.

DESPITE the fact that her work was going well, it was hard to sit at a typewriter on these glowing mornings. One day when Gredge, the gardener lent from Ravensmoor by Mr. Farr, arrived for his weekly stint, Lucia left her desk with the excuse that she ought to initiate a chat and make herself known to him. It was wasted effort. No matter what she said, Gredge responded with "Ah!" shedding an old man's tear which trickled down his seamed russet cheek.

Perhaps like his employer Gredge didn't care for Americans or women or, especially, both in one. Lucia returned to the house, entering the kitchen for coffee at a moment when Mrs. Berry was emptying wastebaskets from upstairs. "Does Gredge talk at all, Mrs. Berry?"

"Oh, aye, but he never did like coming down from Ravensmoor, even for poor Mrs. Farr."

"Poor Mrs. Farr?"

As if she'd made a slip of the tongue, Mrs. Berry gave Lucia a startled glance, and folding her lips in on themselves, she took up her baskets and scurried back upstairs again, leaving Lucia standing there with her coffee mug and her backlog of unformulated, unanswered questions.

Late that afternoon, returning from the superette, Lucia took the path through the churchyard, wending her way past boxwood and holly to the back of the church, where she turned off the path and wandered down a slope among the newer graves.

She came finally upon a little secluded dell, half-hidden by shrubbery ranged in a formal semicircle, and found what she was looking for.

Helen Bellington Farr
wife of Antony Renfrew Farr
Born October 4, 1940
Died March 9, 1982
REST IN PEACE

Sounds from the village were cut off. The encircling shrubs cast a cool shade. Lucia was aware of an intensely private kind of concentration here in this enclosure, as if she were in the presence of someone deep in thought. If she had more acute extra-sensory powers, she felt, if she spoke an untranslatable language, if she were more saintly, perhaps, she might understand what the thought was. It was so close to the surface and so persistent that it all but had utterance. And gradually, it seemed to Lucia, the spirit rapt in concentrated thought changed to one calling mutely for communication, as if, since she'd ventured here, invaded this seclusion, she were being pressed into some kind of service.

At that moment a bird began to sing in the surrounding trees, pouring out a rich, melodious repertoire of phrases, and although Lucia couldn't see the bird, she felt sure it saw her and aimed its song at her.

The effect made her skin crawl, even on the top of her scalp. In such a place, apart from the world, one could imagine almost anything. She was ignorant of the habits of birds, of the fact that they claimed their territory in song, and to her it sounded as if the bird too had taken up the message, whatever it was, importunately demanding, or imploring.

She took a step backwards. *No,* she answered without words. She had burdens enough already, and ghosts of her own to lay to rest.

The bird sang all the more insistently.

No, answered Lucia. I don't understand, I want nothing to do with you!

She wheeled about, turning her back on the grave and the

bird, found the path, and hurried back to the church and the lych-gate that opened on the slope of Church Street. Heart in throat, terrified that the bird might follow, she dragged the gate open and fled down the street.

Miss Morgan was working on her knees in her little plot of garden, transplanting a flat of primroses, and Lucia crossed the street to avoid her. At this moment she didn't need another encounter with her unfriendly neighbor. Heart pounding, she plunged into her house. She had left the bird behind in the churchyard.

Idiot, she told herself, leaning against the inside of her closed door. She had to laugh out loud at herself.

Well, all right; she didn't believe in ghosts, or birds of ill omen, but there was unquestionably a dark side of things pertaining to Bloodrose House, and her own sudden fright had taught her a lesson. Once again she told herself: leave well enough alone. Investigation into the past, as a number of people had hinted, could only lead to distress in the present.

She enjoyed her house; her work was going well; her life had taken a long-overdue turn for the better. She would be well advised to keep it that way.

SIMON telephoned two or three times a week.

At his aunt's luncheon party he'd been too busy making drinks, handing out plates and retrieving them, and in general keeping his eye on his aunts and their guests, to give Lucia his undivided attention, but she enjoyed watching him as with great agility and humor he moved about.

He was not unmindful of her, however. He must have overheard her discussing steak and kidney pie with young Mrs. Winters, who lived next to the rectory. When Lucia made her good-byes he saw her to the door and suggested dinner at an inn in the West Riding where he claimed they made the best steak and kidney pie in Yorkshire. They agreed on the following Thursday.

Whether by design or inspiration he invited his aunts to go, too. He may have thought Lucia would shy at a second date so soon after the first, or think he was working the pilgrimage angle again, but by inviting his aunts along it didn't seem like a date at all. Better for Lucia to wish she were alone with him than wish she weren't! At any rate it turned out to be a hilariously successful evening, and the steak and kidney pie was delicious.

After that it was natural for Simon, like a sort of cousinly well-wisher, to telephone more often.

When he discovered she planned to see York Minster with Peg Goodfriend, he suggested a place to lunch and said he'd love to take them, thus signing Lucia up for another impromptu date. She had to laugh at his ever-so-subtle campaign.

And that was another thing she appreciated about Simon, whether on the phone or in person: he made her laugh.

EVERY afternoon at the end of her day's work she went out for air and exercise. A small door in the back of her garden wall opened onto a lane, and she had found a path leading up from the lane through old orchards and stone walls into rolling sheep-cropped fells, spacious as an open sea, with Ravensmoor looming darkly over them, and this soon became her favorite walk.

The day came when she decided to follow the path all the way to the top of the moor. The weather wasn't promising, but the low-running clouds and little fits of drizzle didn't deter her. She was dressed for just about anything in stout crepe-soled shoes, Irish tweed hat, and raincoat. The damp turf-scented air, in fact, set free her finicky word-bound brain and quickened her blood. Her eyes, too, rid themselves of strain, lifting to the broad sweep of open land, the length and breadth of earth and sky. Sheep, ever-present in a North Yorkshire landscape (in this part of the world hedges and fences were draped with strands of wool), grazed randomly. Lapwings flashed as they rose and settled again, and larks hovered high overhead.

No human sounds or traffic noises reached here, but if one listened carefully one took in a complex chorus—the faint bird cries, the bleat of a sheep far away, and then, as the ear grew more finely tuned, insects stirring, wind moving. As Lucia trudged upward into the rolling wilderness, this all-but-inaudible complexity of sound somehow blended into a mixture of fragrances, of grass and earth, and then sound and scent melted into vision, the miniature daisies underfoot and the expanse of moorland, until at last sight, scent, and sound were all one, part of the feel of the air on her face.

So much pure ozone, Lucia advised herself dryly, could make one a bit daft.

But soon she was bent over, climbing the last dark rise of Ravensmoor, setting one foot after the other. Whoever had worn this path, man or beast, had taken the easiest way up the rise, zigzagging back and forth, but Lucia was winded by the time she reached the stubble of heather. Over'eated also, as Mr. Buckswick would say, and she pulled off her hat and unbuttoned her raincoat and found an outcropping of rock to rest on and enjoy the view.

The whole of the dale was spread below her. The red-tiled roofs of Foxwold nestled in billows of young foliage and flowering hawthorn, with the square tower of St. Wilfred's lifting its four pinnacles high over the pale green foam. Hedges and walls veined the surrounding land, creating a checkerboard of shades of green and russet of newly plowed earth, which undulated away to the long spines of distant misted moors.

She thought of Julian, as she usually did when she was alone and moved by something, the old automatic impulse to share her life with him. She knew he was receding from her, was no longer in the immediate background of all her thoughts, but this in fact didn't cause her to rejoice; getting over Julian, too, had its bittersweet price. Her loss now was not only her love for him, however founded on stubborn, starry-eyed illusion, but her commitment to him. One could always love someone else, she supposed, but perhaps not so willingly and utterly turn over one's life to another. She was not only learning to let go of Julian but to say goodbye to a part of herself.

Well, it was the height of folly and futility to try to work postmortems into a recuperation. Why allow Julian to intrude here in Yorkshire?

She had no ancestral connections with this part of the world but she felt she was by nature attuned to it. She wanted to know all its moods. She wished she might see this valley in winter, blanketed in snow. She wished she might be here in March when the warm spring winds melted the snow and brought up the daffodils. She was glad she was going to have a taste of autumn. The thought of leaving in less than six months gave her a premature pang of homesickness. There was something like the answer to a question here, all questions, the end of a search.

But while she had sat lost in the view it had been growing steadily darker. She glanced over her shoulder and immediately jumped to her feet; a purple squall line was advancing upon her over the crest of the moor like the sliding lid of a box. Hastily she pulled on her hat and buttoned up her raincoat. On the opposite horizon beyond Foxwold she could still see daylight, but here it was turning into night, and she knew she was in for a deluge.

You wanted moods, she told herself in a silent New York accent, you got a mood.

The path she'd struggled up wouldn't be safe or navigable in a downpour, and there was no shelter on the great treeless mound. She had no choice but to find the paved road that traversed the top of the moor and follow it home.

She scrambled farther upward to the crown of the hill, stumbling, tearing her stockings on the wiry heather and scratching her hands as she grabbed for support, while the wind struck her at eye-level and the first stray drops of on-coming rain smacked her in the face. She wasn't afraid. Anxious, perhaps, and exasperated at her clumsiness, but not really frightened as she had been last week in the grave-yard. And in fact she came to the paved road quite quickly.

But there on the top of the moor she met the full force of the squall. It fell on her like a bird of prey, nearly bowling her over. The line of black clouds rushed close overhead, blotting out the last of the remaining light, and the rain took her from all directions, boiling over her ankles and under her skirt, streaming over her face and down her neck. She grasped the brim of her hat with both hands to keep it from flying away, but it was a job to keep her balance. She began to laugh at herself, whirling around drunkenly, try-ing to tell leeward from windward, ducking and skittering along.

She was still laughing when the headlights of a car slanted up over the rise of the road from Foxwold, approaching at a crawl, and, levelling off, slowly bore down on her.

She couldn't flag it down without losing her hat, and since the car was heading away from Foxwold anyway it wouldn't be of much help to her, so she stepped out of the road onto the turf to give it plenty of room.

The car pulled to a halt alongside her, and the window nearest her was lowered.

"What on earth are you doing here?"

It was one of those witless questions people ask in such situations, the question Emerson is said to have asked Tho-reau, in jail for civil disobedience; but it made Lucia bristle. Once more, there was no mistaking that incisive, lordly voice, although the face was blurred. "I'm enjoying a walk," she shouted over the uproar of wind and rain, "and if you're about to order me off your land, I assure you I'm in the process of leaving!"

If he felt moved to retort he restrained himself. The windshield wipers thrashed to and fro. "Get in!" he said. "I'll drive you home!"

The superior tone only goaded her on. She had no wish to be beholden to him. "I wouldn't want to put you out, Mr. Farr!" The tempest seemed to have blown her own self-restraint away, to say nothing of common sense.

He hesitated. He may have had half a mind to take her up on her silly insolence and drive on. Through the shrouds of rain she could only make out the shape of his head, inclined towards her and dimly lighted by the dashboard. "Mrs. Vail," he said patiently, "don't be an idiot. Get in."

Well, of course she *was* being an idiot. How long, she asked herself, did she expect to go on swaying here in this *Walpurgisnacht* pettishly arguing over a reasonable and even kind offer of rescue?

Without another word she swallowed her pride and ran around the front of the car while he unlatched the far door. She plunged in and flung herself into the bucket seat, slamming the door. At once the tumult was shut out and she was in a steamy masculine frowst of leather, damp Burberry, and a faint medicinal odor like sheep-dip. She pulled off her hat and put it out of the way on the floor. "I'm afraid I shall make a great puddle."

He didn't bother to answer. He was already maneuvering the car around to head in the opposite direction. He took his handkerchief to the condensation on the inside of the windshield and, leaning forward to peer through the streaming water on the outside, set off for Foxwold.

"I'm grateful for the ride," she acknowledged more civilly. "I might have drowned standing up."

He didn't smile. "You'll need a hot bath when you get home," he said. "Don't take a chill. You're rather a contentious woman, aren't you?"

She had to laugh again, then, and he gave her a sidelong glance as though catching on that she was slightly unhinged. "Not usually," she told him. "I would say mainly when feeling foolish, such as when caught trespassing, or when soaked to the skin."

"Or," he added, "with someone with whom you've got off on the wrong foot."

She nodded. "Yes, certainly, then too."

They were coming down off the moor now, and the rain was less frenzied, settling into a steady downpour. The darkness had lifted slightly.

Perhaps he had a sense of humor after all, although he still wasn't smiling. In the gray light she could now see one arched black brow, one dark-lashed long-lidded eye, one side of a long nose, and the wine-colored stain filling the slight hollow of one cheek.

"But I came to Yorkshire looking for peace and quietness, Mr. Farr."

"I know, Mrs. Vail." They traveled down the winding grade between hedges and stone walls, and soon they were passing over the humpbacked bridge and entering the lower end of Church Street. "One gets to know quite a lot about one's tenants," he said. "About anyone who lives in the country, for that matter." He drew up before Bloodrose House and turned to her at last with a faint smile, more quizzical than good-humored.

They were basically inimical, she decided; they made bad chemistry. She would have behaved perversely with him even if they hadn't got off on the wrong foot to begin with. A clash between the Old World and the New, perhaps. The upper-class voice, the condescending smile, the feudal intonation when he said "one's tenants" simply rubbed her the wrong way, touching off this uncharacteristic, ungenteel, reckless, go-to-hell response.

"Fix yourself a hot drink," he advised, reaching for his door-latch, preparatory to seeing her to her front door.

"Please don't get out," she told him. "I'll run for it. Thanks for the lift. Good night."

She let herself out, rounded the car, and ran indoors without looking back.

She stripped off her drenched raincoat and shoes in the

kitchen where they wouldn't spot the carpet. She had forgotten her hat. The house felt chilly, and she turned up the thermostat. She sneezed mightly and plugged in the electric tea kettle.

But now that she was safe at home it occurred to her how lucky she was. In retrospect, she felt there was something ominous about the headlights of the car slanting up over the crest of the moor and crawling forward, picking her out where she stood at bay in the rain and wind. What was the message Helen Farr seemed to want to convey from her grave? Lucia wondered if her antipathy to Antony Farr had a more deep-seated basis than mere cultural differences: if it was based, for instance, on fear.

Carrying her mug of hot tea, she padded upstairs to get out of the rest of her wet things. She found she was shivering, and sneezed again.

She wondered if she had been a lot closer to danger than she realized.

THAT night she heard the anguished cry again.

Or thought she heard it. Something, possibly only a dream of a cry, woke her. She sat up in bed.

Because of her shivery condition she had gone to bed with her windows shut and her bedroom door open. But now she felt a strong draft of cold air.

She kept perfectly still, hardly breathing.

If there had actually been a cry, it wasn't repeated. There wasn't the slightest telltale disturbance of the house's normal nighttime silence, other than the curious draft of cold night air.

She swallowed, knowing she had the start in her throat and nose of a real cold.

Inch by inch, she got out of bed, and in her nightgown, with bare feet, crept out to the hall and leaned over the bannister. The cold air stirred about her ankles.

The front door, she was certain, was open.

66

Hadn't she closed it firmly when she came in? But she remembered slamming it shut against the rain, and although here in peaceful Foxwold she wasn't as paranoid about locks as one became in New York, she was almost positive the automatic lock was turned. Perhaps the latch hadn't caught despite the slam.

She was shivering again.

She went back to her room, put on the light and donned her robe and slippers, and with more exasperation than courage, went downstairs.

As she had thought, the front door stood wide open. It had stopped raining, but the wind still flung drops of moisture about in the yawning darkness. She closed the door and this time turned the inside dead bolt. For good measure she bolted the garden doors, and then for her own peace of mind she made a tour of all the rooms, including the upstairs front bedroom.

Nothing was out of order.

Chilled and frightened, she took a cold capsule and got back into bed.

Gray daylight glimmered at her windows before she dozed off again, to sleep fitfully, with menacing, formless nightmares.

· VIII ·

SHE had been brought up to treat a cold by staying indoors and keeping warm, staying in bed if necessary and taking aspirin, but not to go running to doctors for antibiotics, which her mother believed did more harm than good, and it didn't occur to Lucia to alter this program. When Mrs. Berry suggested she call in Dr. Jenna, she wouldn't hear of it.

But after Mrs. Berry left at noon she climbed weakly upstairs, undressed, and got back into bed. Her chest felt sore and creaky, and she knew she was in for more than a case of the sniffles.

The next morning her chest was a cavity of pain. She wasn't interested in breakfast, and at noon Mrs. Berry couldn't tempt her with nourishing soup. This time she gave in and let Mrs. Berry call Dr. Jenna; she felt too ill to argue. His nurse said he would be returning shortly from his morning rounds and would no doubt run in to see Mrs. Vail then.

In fact he came to the house twenty minutes later and Mrs. Berry showed him upstairs.

He wasted no time on breezy bedside amenities, but his thin brown hands were as cool and pacifying as Lucia had guessed they would be. With stethoscope and thermometer he went through the usual examination, only murmuring a brief question now and then. He ordered her to stay in bed, wrote out two prescriptions for Mrs. Berry to fill, said he would be back, and left.

There followed another twenty-four hours which Lucia

didn't remember clearly afterwards. Mrs. Berry was in and out of her room, having announced she was spending the night in the front bedroom, and Dr. Jenna came again at least once. Lucia had never in her life felt so miserable.

But in the course of the third night she awoke in a sweat; her breathing had eased and she knew she'd rounded a corner and was on the mend. In the morning she ate her first breakfast.

"Stay in bed a few more days," said Dr. Jenna, pocketing his stethoscope, "and don't go outdoors for a week. Use up your medication as prescribed. And I shouldn't go walking in the rain again if I were you."

It might be the last time she would see him alone like this. She took the bull by the horns. "Do you remember my telling you about a strange cry in the night?" He was taking up his medicine case, preparing to leave, but her question arrested him and his large, liquid eyes darted to her face. "The other night I thought I heard it again," she said, "and I found my front door had been opened."

He was silent a moment, eyes hooded now, head bowed. When he answered it was in his oblique, enigmatic fashion: "Do you believe in psychic phenomena?"

"I do not, Dr. Jenna." But she wouldn't be surprised if he did. "I tell myself I dreamed the cry and the wind blew the door open."

"But you don't believe that either?"

"No."

He went to one of her two windows and looked down into the garden. "If I were you," he said, "I would bolt my doors and sleep peacefully."

"Shut my ears, you mean, to the cries in the night. To the hints and evasions people make as well. Dr. Jenna, I made up my mind a while ago not to ask any more questions about Bloodrose House, but when these—goings-on actually begin to interfere with my life I think I'm entitled to some answers."

"Do you really believe they would make a difference?"

"At least I might understand!"

"Why should you need to understand?"

He was maddening. "So that I needn't bolt my doors and shut my ears! For instance," she said, her voice dropping. She had broken out in a weak sweat again. "For instance, the way people button their lips about 'poor Mrs. Farr' only points to an untimely end. What sort of end?" Dr. Jenna still stared down into the garden. "One might think she committed suicide, or was murdered."

There was a tiny hiss as he caught his breath and turned to her, the mahogany-colored eyes glittering. "She died of cancer!" he cried softly. "I attended her!"

"Well, there, then," Lucia gave a perplexed sigh, "why is everyone so secretive about that? Is cancer an unmentionable disease here, as it used to be in the States?"

"No!" He made for the door. But he stopped himself on the threshold and turned again. "Helen Farr is at peace. Leave her so!" He made another move to depart and stopped. He said, more evenly, "You are in no condition to trouble yourself about such things. You are a writer. Could it be that you have an overly active imagination?" And before she could retort he continued, "I want to know if there is the slightest change for the worse in your recovery, and I shall want to check you over in a week, before you take up normal outdoor activities. Please ring my nurse for an appointment. Good day." And he left.

She dropped back against her pillows, exhausted.

At least she knew one thing: Dr. Jenna was not as detached, distant, and imperturbable as she had believed.

THE neighbors called or telephoned to inquire after her, sending messages which Mrs. Berry conveyed upstairs. Adelaide Ambrose brought to the door a chicken-and-mushroom pie topped with Olivia's delectable puff-pastry. Peg Goodfriend ran upstairs to leave some paperback whodunits, a bouquet of mixed spring flowers, and a cheerful grin.

70

The following day Lucia was so much improved that Mrs. Berry went home to her sister's across the moor near Farthing, and Bloodrose House was blissfully quiet.

But around three o'clock the door knocker sounded, and hurriedly Lucia put on her warm robe and slippers and with wobbly knees went downstairs.

It was Mr. Slade, Mr. Farr's estate agent, a clean, cadaverous man who was the soul of rectitude but who looked for all the world like one of Dickens's wicked schoolmasters. He blinked at Lucia's attire, obviously not knowing she'd been ill, but his mission was to hand over a plastic shopping bag, the kind that snapped shut at the top. "With Mr. Farr's respects," he said, and bowed, and descended the steps to his bright-blue Mini.

Inside the bag was Lucia's tweed hat.

It had been dried out and stuffed with tissue paper, no doubt the work of a good housekeeper. Lucia removed the tissue paper, hung the hat on its peg in the cupboard under the stairs, and went back to bed.

She exhaled a small puff of annoyance. The return of the hat in a plastic bag, delivered by a retainer, smacked to her of Farrish disdain.

And this incident seemed to trigger a drop in spirits. Perhaps it merely coincided with inevitable post-viral depression. Or with the late-afternoon sunlight, which had reached that hour of rather sad brilliance when in her New York apartment she could if she let herself get a bad case of the lone lorn blues.

There was another knock downstairs. "Damn!" she muttered, and got into her robe and slippers again.

A florist's van with a York address stood in the street, and the driver handed in a huge basket of red hot-house roses. The enclosed card read:

> If this is phthisis thou'rt sickened of,
> Then may thy physic be all my love.
>   Phthsimon

Now that's more like it, she said to herself, laughing. It was a drawing-room-sized basket but she dragged it up to her bedroom.

Once again Simon had worked magic. The lone lorn blues had vanished.

She made one more trip downstairs, to heat up the soup Mrs. Berry had made her and bolt the doors.

There were no disturbances during the night.

SHE was tired of confinement but still a bit weak on her feet, and perhaps it was as well to follow Dr. Jenna's instructions and stay in bed an extra day. She had a hot bath and for the first time put on a little makeup.

In the late morning Mrs. Berry came upstairs to ask if she would see Iris Goodfriend.

"Iris? Of course, I'd be delighted!"

The girl had fashioned herself a miniskirted dress out of an American army tunic belted with a man's tattered tie under which she wore red tights and wooden clogs. But her hair, though frizzy, was not spiked, and she hadn't put on her dead-white makeup. Lucia discovered she had very fair skin, fair hair, and deep violet-blue eyes. Shyly she handed over a paper bag containing Lucia's favorite green grapes.

"Oh, Iris, how dear of you! It's market day, isn't it? Do sit down for a minute, I don't think I'm germy any more. How did you know I love these grapes?"

"I saw you buying them once." Iris took the easy chair in the corner and gracefully crossed her red legs. "You looked so smart. I thought, when I get to be as old as she is I want to look like that, too. Do you suppose they'll have dignified clothes like yours then?"

"Oh, there'll always be something suitable for the elderly."

"Well, you're not elderly, exactly, but you've been *through* everything, sex and marriage and finding your identity and all that. I still have to go through it, and wear punk

72

gear like this, and it seems such a *chore,* and well, *God."*

Lucia shook her head. "Believe me, Iris, there are many things I haven't been through, and some of the things I have been through I've made a poor job of. *Why* must you wear punk gear?"

"What else is there to wear?" wailed Iris helplessly, and Lucia sucked in her cheeks to keep from smiling. Was it true that the young were so restricted? Iris tilted her head, summing up: "You look so . . . so *smoothed out."*

"The smoothed-out look can be protective coloring just as much as punk gear."

"Protective coloring!" echoed Iris, in awe. "Of course, that's what it is!" Her alabaster brow puckered. "I must be sort of old-fashioned, too, like you." She leaned foward confidentially. "You see, I have a weakness for little kids, and they take to me. That's why I do well at school. I'd like to have lots of my own. But then I suppose one really *ought* to have a husband, and that means getting married, and God, the odds against finding the right lad to father a lot of babies are simply insurmountable." Iris did have a vocabulary after all.

"Somehow I think you'll find one," Lucia told her. "But what about the population explosion?"

"What about the atom bomb?" rejoined Iris. "If the world's going to blow up anyway one might as well make the most of it while it lasts. Maybe love will help postpone the blast more than fear."

Lucia had no rebuttal. There was something fundamental about this frizzy-headed Iris, something sturdy as a rock; the blood of Peg Goodfriend, no doubt.

"Well, God," said Iris, "I mustn't wear you out. Philosophizing can't be fun when you're getting over the flu. Mum said you had a near brush with pneumonia." She got to her feet. "What super roses!"

It would be rude and secretive not to reveal the donor. "Simon Myles," said Lucia.

73

"I might have guessed. They *look* like Simon Myles." Iris sighed. "I used to be in love with him when I was a kid." She sighed again and thrust her hands into the pockets of her tunic. "I'll leave you now. But someday when you're better I'd love to settle down to a real talk about *life*."

Lucia, feeling unqualified, didn't especially welcome this project, but she was touched by the girl's trust in her. "Iris, when it comes to knowing something about life, I haven't a patch on your mother."

"But that's the difficulty; she *is* my mother. Sometimes you want to talk with someone who scarcely knows you. Mum knows me too well, and I know she does, and she knows I know she does." Iris giggled, waved a goodbye, and clumped downstairs in her wooden clogs.

Iris wasn't so far behind her mother, thought Lucia. Along with a sense of humor, Iris had wisdom in the making.

Mrs. Berry came upstairs before she left, bringing lunch, the morning mail, and a telephone message of good wishes from Simon Myles.

There was a letter from Lucia's mother saying her old friend Margo Coleman was going over to London in July to stay in her daughter's flat while her daughter and husband, an Embassy official, were on holiday. Margo wanted Lucia's mother to come with her and she, Lucia's mother, had accepted the invitation. Would Lucia like to have her in Yorkshire for a few days?

Her mother would be having her morning coffee about now, preparatory to beginning a quietly industrious day, and Lucia went downstairs and treated herself to a transatlantic phone call. The precise, sensible little voice had always had a bracing effect on Lucia, and it still did. Mental and emotional clutter fell away; a lopsided world righted itself; pain, if any, subsided. Exuberantly she welcomed her mother to Yorkshire, and they chatted for several minutes as they did when Lucia was in New York.

She then spent a peaceful, salutary afternoon in bed, reading a whodunit and eating grapes.

·IX·

NEITHER Lucia nor Dr. Jenna referred to their last, somewhat heated conversation when she went for her checkup in his surgery.

He was as cool and impersonal as ever as his stethoscope traveled over her chest and back. His nurse stood by, forestalling any extraneous talk, and after his examination Dr. Jenna did not invite her to his consulting room. "You may return to normal activity," he told her, "but keep warm and don't tire yourself." He gave her a little bow and left her with his nurse.

There was a finality in his dismissal, thought Lucia, rounding the church as she proceeded up to the square, as if he'd lowered a steel shutter such as storekeepers pull down at the end of the day.

What was he afraid of?

She had a backlog of marketing to do and went from shop to shop, finding the village more crowded now that the summer season was beginning. St. Wilfred's bells chimed four just when she was beginning to tire, so she decided to stop for a few minutes' rest and turned into the Ravensmoor Arms for one of their delectable teas with hot scones and strawberry jam.

The hotel was all a-bustle with tourists. The English crept about like secret agents, but the Americans tramped up and down the creaking, carpeted stairs, addressing each other loudly as if they owned the place. Lucia frowned at herself: It was she who thought she owned the place, resenting the fact that her favorite nook in the small lounge was occupied and Mr. Buckswick was too busy in his office to do more than wave to her. She had to find a corner in one of the larger lounges which were only opened when the hotel was crowded, and it took a long time to order tea. A harried waitress, young and new to Lucia, at last brought the tea tray, flung it down with a clatter, and rushed off.

But the mullioned windows beside Lucia were open to the garden, the room quieted as the Americans drifted away, and the tea was fortifying. And presently she was pleased to see Mr. Buckswick, in a sporty checked suit, coming to join her.

"The rat-race 'as begun," he said with an affable shrug. "And the Festival's yet to come. That's when we get *really* busy! Mind if I sit for 'alf a mo'? 'Ave a sherry with me?" He ordered two sherries, impressing calm with his tone of voice upon the flustered waitress so that she slowed down and went off at a more dignified pace. "Now, then," he said to Lucia, "did I 'ear that you'd been out of sorts? You do look a bit peaky. Miserable business, is 'flu."

"I'm much better," she told him. There was little that Mr. Buckswick didn't 'ear, she was sure. "Dr. Jenna says I'm fit to rejoin the human race."

"And if 'e says so, you are." Mr. Buckswick on his own premises had a way of paying keen attention to what one said while his eyes roved about, automatically checking tea tray, carpet, ashtrays, flowers, and so on. He indicated Lucia's shopping bags. "Looks as if you'd been making up for lost time."

They discussed the busy shops and busy town, thriving on the tourist season, and then Lucia, settling back, crossing her knees and lowering her eyes as she twisted the stem of her glass, said, "Mr. Buckswick, there was a rumor, wasn't there, that Bloodrose House was haunted?"

"No," he exclaimed, his prominent blue eyes widening on her in honest surprise, "*I* never 'eard it!"

"I mean, someone saw lights in the house when it was empty, didn't they?"

"Oh, that." But when Lucia raised her eyes, Mr. Buckswick dropped his. "That would have been Mr. Slade, no doubt, seeing to something."

"At night?"

"Mr. Farr, then."

"He won't set foot in the place."

Suddenly Mr. Buckswick put down his glass, leaned his burly form toward Lucia so that their knees almost touched, and lowered his voice. "Look, luv. Old Crowley and his pal Percival: They're regulars at the pub, they take on a bit of a load—not to disturb the peace, mind, I send 'em 'ome if they look like getting out of 'and, but at best they're not exactly clear-'eaded. Fanciful, they are, dredging up all the old wives' tales of Foxwold and all the old Yorkshire fables. The tourists in the pub love it. Real local color."

Mr. Buckswick glanced over his shoulder for non-existent eavesdroppers. "*They're* the source of those rumors about lights in Bloodrose 'ouse—those two old tosspots! They were *looking* for the occult, see? If they'd seen a dog they'd 'ave turned it into a phantom 'ound of the moors." He sat back in his chair as though triumphantly proving his point. "You wouldn't put any credence in their stories, now would you?"

Lucia studied his florid, good-natured face, while thinking in the back of her mind how interesting it was, here in Britain, where a man could drop his *h*'s and yet use words like *occult* and *credence* with ease. She said, "They saw lights more than once?"

With a barely suppressed sigh Mr. Buckswick fiddled with his glass. It wasn't quite fair to pick him up so sharply on things. "They told the *story* more than once," he answered. "It got attention, made people nod and wink and treat to another round." He gave Lucia a narrow glance. "You 'aven't seen lights yourself, 'ave you?"

77

"No." But she held back now and didn't tell him about the cries in the night and the door opening. If she did tell him he would only smile at her, and then her story too would go the rounds of Foxwold.

He drained his glass and set it aside. "You're American, luv, you're renting the 'ouse for six months. In no time— sad but true—you'll be 'eading back to the States. You don't want to spoil your stay by giving ear to our folk tales. *Unless*," he cried, clapping the arms of his chair and bracing his legs, ready to catapult himself to his feet, "*unless* you're picking up local color to put in a book! Grist for the mill, what? And while we're about it I'd better get back to the grind myself, ha ha!"

"Just one more thing, Mr. Buckswick." He unbraced himself immediately and waited. She hadn't planned how to ask this question but once it had surfaced there was no way to repress it or slip it casually into the conversation. "Has Lady Quelling-Steele been here lately? In the past two weeks?" If anyone had a stray key to Bloodrose House, it would be this presumptuous woman, with a key left over from her decorating job.

"No." Mr. Buckswick shook his head. "She 'asn't been 'ere in a month or more. Not at *my* inn. Sometimes she stops in Harrogate or York." Both Harrogate and York were less than an hour away. But he was curious. "Is something wrong with the 'ouse?"

"Oh, no, thank you, Mr. Buckswick. But, uh, a friend of my mother's who lives in London is looking for, uh," Lucia was not a good liar, "someone to do over her flat. I'll call Mr. Slade."

"Save you the trouble." Mr. Buckswick rose. "Come by my office and I'll give you her business card." Lucia gathered up her shopping bags and followed him out to the lobby. He found the card and she pocketed it. "Can I run you 'ome with those parcels? No? Well, then, drop in again, it's always a pleasure to see you!"

A lot friendlier than Dr. Jenna, she thought, emerging on

the square; but Mr. Buckswick, too, had given her the mind-your-own-business routine.

It seemed far-fetched to imagine Lady Quelling-Steele driving up from Harrogate or York in the middle of the night to harass her, but then Lady Quelling-Steele herself was rather far-fetched. The fact remained: Someone besides herself had witnessed curious goings-on at Bloodrose House, late at night.

WITHOUT thinking she took the shortcut through the churchyard.

Once again it seemed to Lucia that the whole village was involved in a conspiracy of silence. As if they were protecting someone. Or the memory of someone. Poor saintly Helen Farr, for instance.

Or, Lucia told herself with a little start, protecting someone living, someone involved in her death.

The Hon. Antony Farr, local VIP?

Was that the mute but imperative message from her grave?

Lucia had begun to wonder if anyone was quite what he or she appeared to be in Foxwold, and who knew what that he wasn't telling. Besides the mysterious Dr. Jenna, there was a make-believe Admiral and a clergyman who put on a scatter-brained act but whose head, Lucia was convinced, was screwed on as tightly as anyone's in the village, if not more so. There was the impenetrable team of the Ambrose sisters, and their great-nephew, who had his own secrets and might well have been in love with poor saintly Helen. Even Iris went around in disguise.

Lucia laughed out loud, disturbing the hush of the churchyard. *Really.* She was as bad in her own way as besotted old Crowley and Percival (playing parts themselves, like tiresome Shakespeare comics). Dr. Jenna could be right: With her writer's imagination she might be reading things into situations where there was nought to be read.

It was a warm, sultry afternoon and the churchyard hush

was inviting, almost enticing, shutting one away from a jarring, tourist-ridden world. As she passed around the bulk of the church, her footsteps slowed, and then, as if she'd been gravitating in this direction all along, she took the path that led down into the section of newer graves.

She rounded the semicircle of shrubbery and came upon Miss Morgan, on her knees, tidying the grave of Helen Farr.

Miss Morgan looked up with a blazing, trapped expression. They stared at each other, and for an instant there was no escape for either of them.

Lucia took a step backwards, recoiling from the impact of pure, almost tangible hostility, and was about to excuse herself and turn away, but Miss Morgan was rising, trowel in hand. In a low monotone, the lips barely moving, she demanded, "What do you want here?"

"I don't know!" Lucia told her. There was no defense but honesty. "I was deep in thought. I didn't even know I was coming here! Miss Morgan, why do you dislike me so?"

The pale eyes, paler even than Lady Quelling-Steele's, flickered slightly. Honesty apparently disconcerted Miss Morgan, as if it were a weapon, and she seemed to decide to use it herself in retaliation. "They should never have leased her house," she said, her countrified Yorkshire accent out of keeping with her low, spiteful mutter. "They shouldn't have touched it, stripping it and dressing it up, leasing it out to whoever had the price to pay!" She stopped abruptly, pressing her lips together, realizing she wasn't making sense and resenting Lucia the more.

But Lucia understood, at least enough to murmur, "Sacred to the memory of . . ."

"Yes!" cried Miss Morgan, as if freed by these words from restraint. "Yes! What right have *you* to take over her house, make free with it, use her things! An American, not even a decent Englishwoman, a Mrs. without a Mister, flaunting her red hair and her money and right off setting the men to running in and out—!" The more she said, she seemed aware, the more demented she sounded. Again her thin lips clamped shut, and the skin around her mouth whitened. A network of purple veins over her nose and cheeks stood out against the blanched skin, veins like those of a secret drinker. Her head trembled with the intolerable pressure of hatred.

Still keeping her distance, Lucia made a last, misguided attempt to soothe her. "Miss Morgan, I'm really not to blame for being in her house, for stripping it and dressing it up and putting it up for rent."

Miss Morgan raised her trowel like a sword, an angel intercepting blasphemy, a faithful subject defending the lord of the manor. Adrenaline flooded hotly over Lucia's neck and shoulders as she fell back another step. "Whoever is to blame," cried Miss Morgan, cutting Lucia off, "whatever lies on their conscience, they'll be called to account, and it's no concern of yours!" She brought the trowel into line with her nose as if sighting along it. "I've seen him at your door, I've seen you pull up in his car; flirting with him, too, are you?" She took a step forward as if she would drive Lucia all the way out of the graveyard, and Lucia stepped back again. "The fact is, you don't belong here, and he does. Bloodrose House was Mrs. Farr's home and always will be." The trowel shook. "You'd be advised to get out—*now*. Because it won't go well with you. You won't enjoy it."

"But I do enjoy it!"

"You'll see. You'll be glad to leave."

"But why, Miss Morgan?" Lady Quelling-Steele's resentments against Lucia seemed connected primarily with Antony Farr, but Miss Morgan's were centered on the dead Mrs. Farr. *"Why?"*

The trowel descended to Miss Morgan's side, and she wore a little smile. Her voice dropped, sounded more sane, although what she said sounded less so. She whispered: "Because, Mrs. Vail, Bloodrose House has got a curse on it." She was pleased with herself. She showed double rows of even white dentures.

Oh, *honestly*, thought Lucia, exasperated. There was no use arguing with someone who talked of curses. I don't believe it, Lucia told herself. Bloodrose House doesn't feel as if it had a curse on it. At least, it feels as if it didn't *want* to have a curse on it.

Miss Morgan raised her trowel once more. "Get out," she said softly, "before it's too late!"

They stared at each other another second, and then Miss Morgan turned and dropped to her knees before Helen Farr's grave. Savagely she plunged the trowel into the earth and dug at the root of a weed.

And now Lucia realized to her surprise that Miss Morgan was weeping.

"I'm sorry," Lucia told her. "Even though I don't understand, I'm sorry for your suffering."

"Go. Just go."

And Lucia turned and retraced her steps, aiming for the lych-gate, trying not to run.

· X ·

"WHAT we'd better do this morning," said Peg, as they drove south to York, "is concentrate on the cathedral, d'you agree? It's the focal point and glory of the city and all else is secondary. But perhaps if you've already seen it—?"

"Very briefly," said Lucia in the passenger seat, "on my way north from London in April." In April she wasn't really operating on all cylinders. Then, she realized, she viewed everything through the internal blur, or shadow, of her own pain; now, although pain could still be induced by pressure on the scar, the blur between her eyes and the world had miraculously cleared.

It was an external shadow that troubled her in June.

The unpleasant disturbances at Bloodrose House, culminating in her clash with Miss Morgan, haunted her; her brain couldn't leave the unintelligible, unresolvable problem alone. Ghosts and curses! On the one hand it was unreal and absurd; on the other, real and disturbing.

What was it that Miss Morgan, with her melodramatic admonition ("Get out, before it's too late!"), was trying to warn her of?

But today, on her first outing since her recovery from the flu, this cloud cleared also, if only for a few hours. Several times already this morning, without knowing, she'd heaved a sigh of relief. And as they left Foxwold behind and neared York, an eagerness, much like a store of readymade happiness, broke forth within her as if it had been imprisoned, and she viewed the world not only without pain or anxiety but with elation.

"What I want most to do, Peg, is see the cathedral with you."

"Good." Peg smiled. "And we'll try and find another day for a museum or two, and some of the grand old houses. You saw The Shambles, too, I hope? Thank heaven; by June it's overrun with tourists." They were bowling down over the low Howardian hills in the Goodfriends' little estate wagon. "You just can't see York in one day," concluded Peg.

"Perhaps I should have said no to lunch with Simon."

"Indeed not. I'm quite looking forward to the heavenly meal you can be sure he'll provide, but you can also be sure it will take up half the afternoon."

Disposing of the car in one of the public car parks near the medieval gates of the walled city, they climbed to the broad pedestrian walk on top of the ancient wall itself, a more fitting approach to the 600-year-old cathedral towering ahead than the traffic-congested road below, and crossed the River Ouse. From there they proceeded up the street to the glowing golden mass of York Minster.

As Lucia had anticipated, Peg Goodfriend was the perfect cathedral guide. She suggested they first sit down in the center of the nave where they could take in the sheer size and serenity of the place, the soaring alabaster columns and gracefully joined arches. It was not a gloomy cathedral but a joyous one, full of light, especially since its cleaning in the '70s, yet filled too with the rapture, the mysticism, of medieval church achitecture.

While they sat, an organist far forward began to practice, trying out trumpet blasts, tumultuous arpeggios, and earth-shaking rumbles that reverberated all over the great edifice and gave Lucia an uplifting thrill.

Peg knew her reredos and rood screens, her triforiums and sacrariums, but she wasn't a bore or a show-off, and after they got to their feet again she pointed out details Lucia might have missed—the lovely gilt bosses high overhead, the shields of fourteenth-century noblemen who had stopped here on their way to the Scottish wars, the more ancient panels of stained glass. The great east window, Peg mentioned, was the size of a tennis court.

Slowly they circled the building, looking into chapels, examining tombs and memorials. The organ workout led into a rehearsal of the choir, the boys' pure voices soaring into the reaches of the vaulted ceiling and setting the resonance chambers of Lucia's own head to tingling. Near the south door, Peg waited while Lucia donated a pound note for which she would in time receive an engraved citation, testifying that she'd contributed to the upkeep of the cathedral for two minutes.

And then it was time to move on to lunch.

In Europe, Lucia had noted, fine restaurants were usually distinguished not by lavish decor and an uproar of glittering patrons, as in New York, but by a subdued and dedicated shabbiness. Simon was waiting for them in such an establishment, occupying the second (or as the Europeans would have it, the first) floor of a slightly sunken Renaissance house, its leaded windows deep-set, its dark velvet upholstery worn, its paneling black with age. As for the patrons, they too were of a certain splendid shabbiness, with the look of terrible fussbudgets who never compromised, but the noise they made was no more than a discreet buzz, as in a private club. The only one in the room who might have passed as glittering was Simon himself, who was at his attractive, well-dressed best, and who seemed suddenly to Lucia, after not seeing him for several weeks, quite irresistible. It was that kind of day, when everything moved her, warmly and happily.

Preceded by a ceremonious head waiter, Simon ushered them to a choice table in a corner. Circumventing any nonsense about ordering omelettes or chicken salad, he said he'd taken the liberty of ordering for them, and at once a retinue commenced pouring wines and serving a succession of delicate, miniature courses, leading one from the other without a gastronomical jolt.

Unabashedly Simon studied Lucia's face. "There's something other-wordly about her since the flu," he said. "She's not wasting away, is she? A touch of phthisis?"

"Judging by the way she's tucking into the poached salmon," replied Peg, "I should judge not."

"This isn't poached salmon," Lucia told them blissfully. "This is edible art. As Iris would say, *God!*"

"How *is* Iris?" Simon inquired. "What's the latest fad?"

"She's undergoing some kind of transition," said Peg. "I tremble to think what may come next. She's cool to her helmeted, leather-clad admirers. She's not wearing any makeup at all; she's not oiling her hair, or whatever she does to it. She did say she'd like a plain denim skirt like Lucia's."

"Good lord, Iris in a skirt!" cried Simon. "And wanting

to look like Lucia!" He gave Lucia his semi-serious, deep-blue-eyed regard. "Commendable," he said quietly, "but hardly feasible."

"Maybe," said Lucia, "the time has come when she wants to look like Iris Goodfriend."

Peg's face brightened. "Now that *would* be interesting. I don't really know what Iris *does* look like."

They all three laughed, at Peg more than Iris, and thus amiably they progressed through Simon's ambrosial lunch.

Afterwards he insisted they come and see his shop before they started home to Foxwold. He might have sensed that Lucia wouldn't really know him until she glimpsed the man of business behind his facade of carefully cultivated frivolity.

She had imagined a quaint, bow-windowed Olde Curiositie kind of place, such as lined The Shambles, but Simon's "shop" turned out to be a tall Regency house, spanking white with shining black ironwork and windowboxes of brilliant geraniums. The first two floors were showrooms for his collection of Georgian and Empire furniture, displayed tastefully in their appropriate rooms, so that a new customer might think he'd walked into an elegant private home by mistake, but for the discreet tap of a typewriter in a rear office and the appearance of a gracious salesperson. The floor above was used for storage, and the top floor, which they reached by a small lift, served as Simon's "digs."

"My escape from the eighteenth century," he told them, switching on recessed lights and conducting them into a mirrored living room. A great unframed canvas of almond-colored paint splashed with vermilion glowed under a spotlight on one wall. He showed them the rest of the flat, the red library, the bedroom with a fur spread on the commodious bed (large enough for two, or even three), the tiny stainless-steel kitchen.

Back in the living room he invited them to rest a moment, but Peg said she thought they'd better not as Cedric needed the car, and would Simon mind if she telephoned him to say they were on their way? She went off to the library, and Simon joined Lucia where she stood gazing at the painting.

He took her hand companionably, and she turned to him. "Simon, I'm impressed. You must have a clientele of dukes and duchesses."

"They come to sell, poor dears, not to buy," murmured Simon, still holding her hand. "My clientele consists of a few conglomerate moguls, half a dozen anonymous Americans, and two rock stars. And let us not forget to praise Allah for the Arabians." He went on with scarcely a pause, "I'm coming up to take my aunts to a Festival concert at Farthing next Tuesday—one of those rather precious programs of early English music played on ancient instruments. But it's quite nice at Farthing, in a fine old barrel-vaulted room. Will you go with us?"

"I'd love it." She added, "Come and have supper with me, all of you. I'll use my dining room for the first time."

"Lovely." His eyes held only a token of their usual amusement. "But someday I should very much like to have you to myself again. It's about time, don't you think?"

"Perhaps so, Simon." There was a slight catch in her voice, for although it might have been her own wanton imagination she seemed to feel a strongly sensual warmth passing from his hand to hers.

Then Peg returned, and he accompanied them downstairs and kissed them goodbye, and soon they were heading north again.

"He has such a sweet way of making you think your every wish is his command, hasn't he?" said Peg. "When all the while he's managing everything himself."

Lucia nodded; he did.

"I'm not used to that," Peg confessed. "I manage Cedric, I'm afraid." Lucia privately thought Cedric might require considerable management, but Peg cocked her head on one side. "Or do I? D'you suppose all these years Cedric, too, has been letting me *think* I'm managing?"

"Whoever is letting who think what, it's obviously working well for you. Perhaps only people who love each other very much can spare each other from their own frailties, if you know what I mean."

"Yes, I do, Lucia. The key word, of course, the thing on which the rest hangs, is love."

"Amen."

"Although there *are* frailties," said Peg reasonably, "it would be the height of folly to accept."

"I guess so. Like one's husband having affairs with other women." Lucia gave a little muffled laugh. "I'm learning so much more about marriage now that I'm not married than I did when I was married."

"Does it help to talk about it?" Peg wasn't a clergyman's wife for nothing; if there was anything she knew how to do well it was to listen to other people's troubles.

"Sometimes," replied Lucia cautiously, meaning it depended on the time and place and especially the person. And because Peg kept silent Lucia did begin to talk, haltingly but honestly, really the first time she had leveled with any woman. The countryside unfolded under fat June clouds, and some of Lucia's life unfolded with it as they rolled along— her conventional, comfortable, proper background and her conventional efforts to break away from it, her job with a New York publishing firm, where Julian was on his way to the top. What on earth did he see in her, she used to ask herself, besides her hair, which had attracted him in the first place? But from her present, more detached viewpoint she had to face the fact that he must have seen too the comfortable background. He may have thought he was marrying a rich man's daughter when, alas, he was really marrying a romantic idealist, too naive to see his frailties, let alone accept them, too proud to take money from her father. The marriage, she told Peg, began to fail from the moment it took place.

She broke off with another laugh. "I was going to pump *you*, Peg, about Bloodrose House, and here I am emptying skeletons from my own closet!"

"And I am honored," said Peg simply. She was silent for a long while, and Lucia thought the time of intimacy had come to an end. But Peg said at last, "What do you want to know about Bloodrose House?" Her voice was different. No one, it seemed, was happy talking about Bloodrose House.

Lucia took a deep breath. It was a wrench even for her to let go once more of the irrevocable past and take up the unaccountable present. "All right: Why the veiled silences? What do they veil?"

"Ah."

"Why does everyone say Ah?"

Peg made a sound that was half-laugh, half-sigh. "In a nutshell: Helen Farr died there, after a long losing battle with cancer. Tony left the house to go back to Farthing and never returned."

Lucia waited a moment and then asked, "That's not all, Peg, is it?"

Peg was silent again, and Lucia thought she wasn't going to answer, and then, reluctantly, Peg forced out, "There was gossip. It was suggested her death was hastened."

Lucia herself said, "Ah." It was true: Everyone suspected someone. Lucia decided she might as well go the whole way while she had the chance. "Hastened by Dr. Jenna?" In spite of herself she pictured Dr. Jenna, cool and slim, bending with a hypodermic needle over a wasted, tormented frame in the front bedroom. No wonder he was so touchy, on the defensive when Helen Farr's name was brought up. Even if he was perfectly innocent, Helen Farr was his responsibility, and the veiled hints would have outraged him.

"Not necessarily," said Peg. "He tried everything to save

her. The rumor was, before she died, that he was even willing to try some uncertified miracle drug from the States and had sent for it. Lucia, any number of people could have done it. We were all in and out of the house the day she died—the Ambrose sisters, Cedric and I, even Simon and Will Luddington."

"And Tony Farr, too, of course?"

"Of course!" Peg had become increasingly unhappy over the subject.

"Why do people suspect her death was hastened?" Having got this far with her questions, Lucia couldn't stop. "Was there some telltale evidence? I mean, if Dr. Jenna certified she died of cancer . . . unless you mean he deliberately overlooked something?"

Peg was silent. That in itself was telltale. She gripped the wheel tightly as if to stop a tremor.

Lucia tried another tack. "Where did Miss Morgan come in?"

"She was Helen's nurse."

"Was she!" exclaimed Lucia. "Yes, I remember now: Adelaide told me she was a good nurse. Could *she* —?"

"Lucia, I'll name no one! I blame no one!"

"Or Antony?"

"What difference does it make?" Peg cried out. Color fired her cheeks. "Death was a blessing, whether it came too soon or too late!"

"Was she near death anyway?"

"She must have been!" With an effort Peg lowered her voice. "I like to think, no matter whose doing it was, God's or some poor desperate human's, or for what reason, that it was an act of mercy."

"She was greatly loved, wasn't she?"

That seemed to undo Peg. Tears sprang to her eyes and fell out on her cheeks, and she brushed them away with the bent knuckles of her index finger. "Enough, Lucia! Please, no more. It's a painful subject, you know that!"

"All right. I'm sorry." But she wondered at Peg's agitation. She was almost as overwrought as Miss Morgan had been. It wasn't like this solid, self-possessed woman to shed tears so helplessly.

Surely it couldn't be that something weighed on Peg Goodfriend's conscience?

They both fell silent. They were nearing the turn-off for Foxwold, and Lucia's shadow of dread had returned.

Love was the key word. But Lucia's mind was wrestling with intimations, vague clues she hardly knew she possessed. She had an unformulated, unsubstantiated feeling that she'd just now come close to uncovering something ugly and sinister, if not criminal.

Something Peg knew more about than she could tell.

In the absence of love, thought Lucia, there was no mercy.

And in that case the key word would be *murder*.

· XI ·

THE blue skies and fat cumulus clouds of June prevailed, and Festival Week promised to open to perfect weather.

Nothing untoward had happened at Bloodrose House and the feeling of foreboding had shrunk to the back of Lucia's mind, although it had by no means vanished. She had no intention of being misled by this peaceful interval, and she was careful with locks and bolts. Occasionally she awoke in the night and listened.

In spite of herself she waited, without knowing what she waited for.

As for Miss Morgan, who had declared her resentment, Lucia glimpsed her bent over her flower beds or disappearing up the street, but in fact they didn't come face to face.

IT was market day and very warm, even for Lucia. She was chatting with Will Luddington at her favorite fruit stall when out of the blue over the bustle of the market came the celestial sounds of flutes and violins.

Stopping in mid-sentence, she stared at the Admiral. "Am I hearing things?"

He pointed to the open windows of the Town Hall. "It's one of the Festival ensembles rehearsing upstairs."

"Of course! The Festival begins tomorrow, doesn't it? How delightful! I've never marketed to Mozart."

The Admiral let out a great guffaw, startling the townspeople around them and exciting Bertie to bark. "Marketing to Mozart!" he chortled. And Lucia left him repeating the phrase to his fellow Foxwoldians.

She happened on yet another rehearsal as she rounded St. Wilfred's on her way home: Out of the open panes of the arched windows spilled a sumptuous abundance of notes from the inexhaustible cornucopia of Johann Sebastian Bach. It was certainly not the diffident playing of Beryl Pillin, St. Wilfred's organist; this robust have-at-it style was of York Minster caliber. Lucia retraced her steps around the retaining wall (playing it safe, she'd given up using the shortcut through the churchyard) and went up the front walk, intending to sit down somewhere in the shade under the open windows. But the double south door was open wide, and approaching cautiously, Lucia found no barriers or notices against going inside; in fact one or two people were already seated in the gloom, listening.

She entered on tiptoe and slid into the nearest pew.

Her musical education had followed the accepted routine

of her upbringing—a few piano lessons as a child, a music appreciation course in school, odd Friday afternoons at the Philharmonic for a season or two, and an occasional evening at the opera. The complexities of Bach were beyond her grasp, but with her innate sensibilities she could sit in his presence and be stirred to the roots of her being along with the better educated.

The sunlight filtering through the trees outside filled the building with a shadowy greenish light, and it was cool, and the cascade of organ notes tumbled over the handful of listeners like a waterfall in a ferny glen.

Now and then the invisible organist paused to repeat a passage or perhaps to pencil a note, and it was during one of these abrupt silences that Lucia realized she was contemplating the quarter-profile of Antony Farr. He was sitting two or three rows ahead of her on the other side of the center aisle, his eyes shut and his arms folded, not unlike one of the long-nosed effigies of his ancestors scattered about the church. But for the nose and the arch of the brows he might have been any Yorkshire farmer, in an open shirt with the sleeves rolled up, although perhaps few Yorkshire farmers could take the time to sit quietly, even humbly, listening to Bach.

There sat a man imprisoned in sorrow, or guilt. Lucia studied the immobile shuttered face with the carved cheekbones as if seeking in it an answer to Foxwold's private riddle.

Had this man put Helen Farr to death?

He opened his eyes and frowned as though his dreams had been disturbed, and Lucia, sensing he would in the next instant find her eyes on him, took up her shopping bag and slipped out as she had come in. The organ notes pealed forth again as she headed down the walk.

"Mrs. Vail." A step sounded behind her.

It was like a command: Stop where you are. Attend to me.

But Lucia, determined that this time she wasn't going to let herself react with undignified truculence, turned and smiled. "Yes, hello, Mr. Farr."

He approached in the dappled sunlight, and halting alongside her looked down over the churchyard wall and the multicolored awnings of the market stalls. "You might call me Tony," he told her, with an offhandedness that ruffled her despite her resolve. "Everyone else does."

"All right. And I'm Lucia."

"I heard you caught cold after all."

"Yes." He was bronzed by the sun, and his hair, eyebrows, and lashes glistened like jet, as though freshly showered. Once more, as he kept his eyes on the busy market, she compared him to Simon—the blonde and the brunette, the affable and the unaccommodating, the open and shut. But she was staring again, she realized, and she, too, turned to the market. "It didn't last long," she told him.

"Slade said you looked ill when you came to the door. You didn't take my advice, did you?" A dark, sardonic glance came part way, but not all the way, to her face. Why this sudden shyness, she wondered—if it was shyness? He certainly hadn't avoided looking her in the face when he ordered her off his land, or into his car out of the rain.

"Yes, I did," she answered, "and I had a dollop of brandy in my tea besides. It didn't do any good." No need to go into the matter of roaming about the house in the cold at midnight. "The damage was already done."

"I'm sorry." He turned finally and looked at her at last, but distantly, casually, as one looks at an acquaintance of no special interest. Her own eyes turned questioningly to meet his, for he'd surprised her with his word of sympathy, however neglible, and then as if by common consent they looked away again. Why this shyness on *both* sides?

She revived her good intentions. "It's really quite exciting, isn't it?" she began brightly, giving him her most charming smile, even though, again, he wasn't looking at her. She was determined all at once to shake him out of his somber preoccupation, to get some sort of response from him without being contentious. "I mean, it isn't often that one goes marketing with Mozart coming from one side of the square and Bach from the other!" If the remark had made a hit with the Admiral, it might work with Tony Farr.

He didn't even smile.

Oh, well, she thought; so what.

And she fell into a flat sort of sadness, here in the lovely green shade of June, without knowing whether it was a childish feeling of rejection or a natural reaction to a man locked in secrets. She might better remember that after their previous encounter she'd sensed danger.

Discouraged, she moved on down the walk.

He moved with her, accompanying her to the gate. She looked up with a last smile, this time uncontrived, a smile of defeat and acceptance. "Goodbye." She didn't feel it necessary to add his newly proffered first name.

He kept his hand on the gate, not exactly barring her way but delaying her, as if about to reveal yet another side of himself.

"If I'd known you were ill I'd have sent something more appropriate, from the greenhouse," he told her, and there again was the amused glance he'd given her in his car, transforming the bleak and haughty face, quickening it with possibilities, not only of humor but of sensitivity and warmth. "Instead of your own hat."

He opened the gate for her, followed her out, gave her a salute with one finger to his brow, and turning on his heel, paced away in the direction of the market.

FESTIVAL Week opened officially the next day. Busloads of patrons were disgorged in the square, and cars were parked on every street and side street. Lodgings were booked solid. A number of private residences turned themselves into temporary Bed & Breakfast accommodations, and the warmth of many a sitting room in January was paid for in June. Even the rectory took in a few strays, free of charge, although a donation to St. Wilfred's was suggested. Young people with serious musical tastes camped out in fields alloted to them, where they made miniconcerts of their own, and when smoke of a suspiciously pungent nature wafted over the hedgerows the overworked police averted their nostrils. The Admiral's little beige Bertie, head thrust through the railings in front of his house, barked at passing strangers. Mrs. Berry said she wished she had a pound note for every tourist who stopped to photograph Bloodrose House, ablaze now with roses.

The commotion reached Lucia only faintly, at work at the back of the house. The soft warm weather was holding, and the glass doors were open wide to the fragrance of the garden.

At four she stopped and stretched, thinking about her afternoon cup of tea and a walk on the moor, when there was a single sharp bang of the front door knocker.

Adelaide, she thought. She was beginning to identify individual knocks—Adelaide's powerful bang, Peg's businesslike rap, Iris's shy one, Will Luddington's brisk rat-tat, Gladys-the-postman's rat-tat-tat, and any number of anonymous knocks which she knew were those of tradesmen.

It wasn't Adelaide.

This time the door was bolted. Lucia opened it to Lady Quelling-Steele.

"Wanted to have a bell installed," said the lady without preliminaries, "but Tony wouldn't hear of it. Rather fun, the odd battle of wills with Tony. Not a little, humm, erotic." Once again she said, more in demand than query, "May I come in."

With a wry smile, not quite trusting herself to say anything at all, Lucia opened the door wider and stepped aside.

Lady Quelling-Steele was wearing gray suede today,

when the hardy women of Foxwold were wearing sleeveless cotton dresses. It was becoming to her silver-blonde hair, and again unbidden she stripped off outerwear, tossed it on the hall chair, and proceeded with long strides into the sitting room.

"It *is* rather sweet, isn't it? she crooned, pivoting, her silky suede skirt eddying to and fro. "There was nothing one could do, actually, but drown it, simply sub*merge* it, in roses." She turned a lamp around and moved a flower bowl an inch or two. "Otherwise one would end up with the same dreary little room. Harness brasses, she went in for, my dear, and warming pans." Lucia assumed that *she* meant Helen Farr and *my dear* was a figure of speech used like *humm* for emphasis. "You've put real roses about, how clever of you."

"I was just going to make myself a cup of tea," said Lucia, ignoring the mock-compliment. "Would you care for one?"

Lady Quelling-Steele folded her thin arms and assumed her suppressed-amusement expression, like an adult trying vainly to keep a straight face for a child, and appeared to give the question her most profound consideration. "Yes!" she exclaimed at last. "Actually I would!"

"I'll put the kettle on," said Lucia levelly. "I won't be a moment. Do sit down."

But as before Lady Quelling-Steele had driven up from London and was tired of sitting. "I'll use the loo actually and wander about. Weak tea with lemon." And so saying she more or less guided Lucia out to the hall and took herself upstairs.

Sucking in her own cheeks, Lucia made tea, thankful she happened to have a lemon, knowing perfectly well Lady Quelling-Steele was enjoying an agreeable snoop upstairs. Lucia wished one of her pretty nightgowns were hanging on the back of the bathroom door instead of the much-laundered flannel granny-gown that kept her warm at night. Actually, as her guest would say, Lucia was entertained by her more than provoked, and wondered what she'd get up to next. And what did she mean when she said controversy with Tony was erotic?

Returning with the tea tray to the sitting room, she discovered Lady Quelling-Steele had come downstairs and gone out to the garden where she stood in moody contemplation of the flower beds, packed now with all manner of colorful blooms.

"Would you like to have tea outside?" called Lucia from the open study doors.

Lady Quelling-Steele whirled about and considered, tongue in cheek, making Lucia hold the tray and wait on her decision. "Let's!" she cried, bringing the palms of her hands together. "We'll have a little tea party under the tree, shall we?" And she went and flung herself down in one of the rustic chairs and patted the table beside her.

Without offering assistance she watched Lucia come carefully down the two steps, cross the lawn and settle the tray. Then, her lips puckered irrepressibly, she let Lucia pour her tea and sat sipping it in silence, her eyes traveling with amusement over Lucia's workaday cotton polo shirt and denim wrap skirt.

If she was waiting for Lucia to break the silence, Lucia wasn't aware of it. Lucia took sustenance from silence. The warm fragrance of the garden was a voice in itself, and she hoped it might work its peaceful spell on this tense and brittle woman.

But Lady Quelling-Steele's long, beautifully shod foot began to nod restlessly up and down, and at last it was she who felt forced to speak, with an impertinence all the more studied. "Odd you don't use the front bedroom," she said. "It's so much roomier, actually. Why don't you?"

Lucia smiled. "Because I see someone in that big bed wearing a marabou jacket and eating chocolates—that is, when not engaged in steamy *fin de siècle* sex. I'm more the Liberty print type."

It was not an answer intended to take the wind out of Lady Quelling-Steele's sails, but it seemed to have that effect. "Obviously," she rejoined, which was not up to her standard. Her eyes were as bright and furious as Miss Morgan's, but whereas Miss Morgan's were fanatical, Lady Quelling-Steele's were fiercely calculating, constantly weighing advantages and disadvantages, which Lucia uneasily sensed was an indication of treacherous insecurity.

Quickly Lucia tried to make peace before it was too late. "What was the front bedroom like before you redecorated it?"

"Oh, dismal." Lady Quelling-Steele shrugged and turned to Gredge's knife-edged flower beds. But in fact it was a good question, enabling her to exploit what she could do best. "Brown, like the rest of the house, that dismal warm brown—brown wallpaper, brown trim, brown velvet draperies. They had some rather good antiques, but she used them so unimaginatively that they looked like shabby second-hand furniture." Her nostrils flared contemptuously. "Just what you'd expect from a girl who never wore makeup. *And* I daresay never went in for steamy *fin de siècle* sex, as you put it . . . Although one never knows with these pure women, does one?" And she gave Lucia a sweeping head-to-toe glance to make her disdain perfectly clear.

But Lucia had come wide awake. "You knew her? Mrs. Farr?"

"Oh God, I went to school with her!"

Breathlessly Lucia waited (what did that Oh God mean?), but Lady Quelling-Steele, with a puff of the nostrils, fell silent. It was her vehemence that had alerted Lucia. Peg Goodfriend had sounded the same note, and Dr. Jenna. Miss Morgan, for that matter. Antony Farr, crying *"No!"* when Lucia perfunctorily invited him in. Poor saintly Helen Farr hadn't left anyone unmoved or indifferent.

Impulsively Lucia leaned forward. "What was she like?"

Perhaps if she'd been less direct, less beseeching, woman to woman, leaving herself less open for a snub, she might have got an answer. But Lady Quelling-Steele closed her eyes haughtily and drawled, "She was an old friend. I wouldn't dream of discussing her with a stranger."

Baloney, thought Lucia, in New Yorkese. Lady Quelling-Steele wasn't a woman of compunction. But Peg Goodfriend didn't want to talk about Helen Farr either, she actually wept. Lucia slumped back, frowning across the shaded lawn. "Were you exorcising her ghost," she asked, "when you did over the house?"

"What an idea!" scoffed Lady Quelling-Steele. But it intrigued her. "Tony gave me a fairly free hand, when in fact I wouldn't have been surprised if he'd forbidden me to enter the hallowed bedroom at all. I'm quite sure he hasn't been in the room *or* the house since she died! Moved right back to Farthing and stayed there!" Her closed fist suddenly banged the table, rattling the tea things. "If only I'd been able to persuade him to come back to Bloodrose House, just once, and see how *different*—!"

She cut the plaintive cry short. She turned on Lucia once more as if she were the handiest target. "And now *you're* in it! Tell me, *Mrs.* Vail. I notice you don't wear a ring. Are you looking for a new husband?"

Lucia, aghast, said the first thing that came into her head. "Not at the moment." Hadn't she heard somewhere that Lady Quelling-Steele and Tony Farr had had a falling out?

The silver-gray eyes gleamed, smoldering. "Too bad you're American, and not just a *little* more, humm, alluring, otherwise Tony might be a good catch for you, mightn't he?"

Ah, so that was what was bothering her, had been ever since she marched in the door the first day. Lucia decided she'd better straighten this out at once. She put aside her cup and looked the lady in the eye. "Lady Quelling-Steele, if you are interested in Tony Farr yourself, you have nothing to fear from me. He's not my type nor am I his, and anyway, as you must already know, you have a far more powerful rival than I, and her name is Helen Farr."

For a moment Lady Quelling-Steele didn't move a muscle. Then, very slowly, her head turned to the flower beds. "As always," she began softly, as if to herself. "*Always*. At school; in London during the season; in the country at house parties. *Her* blonde hair was natural, *her* peaches-and-cream complexion, *her* long eyelashes, were real!" Lady Quelling-Steele's voice rose. "Always first, captain of the team or president of the club or head of the committee! What's more, the richest—all those millions from the chocolate factory! And so *good*, so *kind! She* got Tony, even though he was second-best, since George was already married—and no one else stood a chance!" Lady Quelling-Steele dropped her head back and sent skyward a sound halfway between a laugh and a sob. "Even *dead*, she wins!"

She leaped to her feet. "I must get back to the Arms. Rodney will be fretting." And with Lucia almost running after her, she strode through the house, grabbed up her coat, scarf, and gloves, and went out the door.

Once again she paused on the threshold, but she kept her back to Lucia. "You'll be going to the concert at Farthing, I suppose?"

Lucia could figure this out too now: The concert was Lady Quelling-Steele's opportunity—if not contrivance—to run into Tony again. She wasn't convinced that she had nothing to fear from Lucia. She would prefer to have the field to herself.

"Yes," Lucia told her gently.

The thin shoulders lifted in another shrug and fell, and without a word or a backward glance Lady Quelling-Steele went down the steps to her silver Jaguar. There was a glimpse of leopard-skin upholstery as she got into the car, and then with a couple of imperious starts and reverses she made a U-turn in the middle of the street and drove back to the square.

Quietly Lucia closed the door. She didn't enjoy causing discomfort. She was, unlike Helen Farr, a poor winner.

She went back to the garden to gather up the tea things.

★   ★   ★

In June the sun didn't set until late in the evening, and Lucia had no qualms about walking alone on the open fells in broad daylight. But an uneasiness followed her on her walk nonetheless, something troubling left over from the visitation of Lady Quelling-Steele, besides a renewed worry about the possibility of another disturbance in the night at Bloodrose House. It wasn't until she was nearly home again that she remembered something Lady Quelling-Steele had told her: Helen Farr had had millions.

Tony Farr would have stood to gain, greatly, by her death.

· XII ·

The small yellow dining room looked pretty, Simon and his aunts were generous with praise for Lucia's cooking, and as usual they had a good time together.

When Lucia had first set eyes on these three, they had been laughing, coming arm in arm out of the house next door, and she had felt a wistful pang of envy. Now all four of them left Bloodrose House in the same way—two by two, arm in arm, laughing.

Anyone watching them, thought Lucia ruefully, like the lonely woman across the street who apparently missed nothing, might feel the same pang.

But Lucia was light of heart this evening. There had been no disturbances the night before, and she dared to think they'd come to an end. Arriving at Farthing, she forgot them altogether and stood under the time-bronzed facade with its tall, many-paned windows, her own species of extra-sensory perception stirred not only by the dignity and beauty of the great house but also by its personality, its mute eloquence, its five-hundred-year-old wisdom.

There was no time to dwell on it. A stream of music-lovers carried her with Simon and his aunts into an immense paneled hall and on toward a broad staircase leading up to the gallery where the concert was traditionally given.

On one side of the hall, out of the babbling main-stream, a group of men and women in evening dress, readily identifiable as Festival officials, were ranged loosely alongside their host, Antony Farr, like an informal reception committee, flatteringly deferring to him and now and then throwing back their heads with mirth at what must have been a touch of humor on his part. Nevertheless, despite the fact that Antony Farr wore his slight smile and looked at ease in evening dress, no one could tell for sure whether he was amused or pleased or bored to death. His face brightened at sight of the Ambrose sisters and he nodded to them, but one of the Festival committee claimed his attention and as he bent an ear his eyes passed over Lucia and his expression lapsed into enigma again.

Simon was chatting on about the annual epidemic of festivals in Britain, and they were halfway up the stairs when Lucia looked down to see Lady Quelling-Steele making her entrance.

A current of interest ran instantly over the crowd, and although no one actually stopped talking in mid-sentence, the babble of voices fell noticeably in volume.

Head high, superb in folds of a gossamer gray Oriental fabric shot with silver and gold, Lady Quelling-Steele swept into the hall, followed by a shorter, younger man, like a page, clad in black and white satin, trotting on tiptoe to keep up with her. Rodney, no doubt, thought Lucia.

Lady Quelling-Steele paused on the threshold, not only

giving every eye time to take her in, but casting an eagle eye herself over the crowd. Then, spotting Antony Farr at the other end of the hall, she lifted her hands limply and gracefully, palms down, tilted her head, pursed her lips in a mischievous *moue,* and with little gliding steps which left her head perfectly level but caused her gown to float out behind her, made for him.

Perhaps he knew she was in town, was prepared for her, and in any case wouldn't allow himself to show the least sign of inhospitality or embarrass a lady in public. For to his undeniable credit, while the committee around him hemmed and hawed and exchanged impenetrable glances and the entire throng of non-staring English somehow managed to take it all in, he received the proffered hands in his and smiled, bent to kiss the cheek she archly presented, said something to her that made her gaily laugh, and then, glancing at his watch, urged her along to the stairs, nodding reassuringly.

She let him go at last. Rodney, who had been pouting at her elbow, was taken in tow again and they mounted the staircase.

"Bravo!" breathed Lucia. The whole thing had gone off so well—Lady Quelling-Steele's perfectly executed maneuver and Tony's perfect manners.

"Yes, you have to hand it to her," agreed Simon. They had reached the top of the stairs, with Olivia and Adelaide just ahead of them, and were following the crowd into the Long Gallery. "Good old Eunice! Never say die!"

"What happened between Eunice and Tony the first time?" asked Lucia.

Simon surrendered his tickets to Iris Goodfriend, one of a bevy of volunteer ushers, who conducted them gravely down the aisle between the rented chairs. The room was nearly filled, the long windows open to the night.

"In answer to your question," said Simon when they were all seated, "nothing. That was the trouble."

"She sent him a bill for twenty thousand pounds, that's what happened!" interjected Adelaide in a voice that, but for the general hubbub, would have carried the length of the gallery. "And love flew out the window!" She began greeting friends with waves and nods, nudging Olivia to make sure she didn't miss anyone.

Lady Quelling-Steele sailed magnificently past with Rodney, to be seated near the front of the room, and Lucia in a simple blue linen dress had to admit there were times when being the Liberty print type left a lot to be desired.

"Now I can tell you," muttered Simon while his aunts on his left conversed with neighbors, "how exceedingly pretty you look."

She brightened. "Simon, you have a genius for saying the right thing at the right moment. I was just then feeling under-dressed and overshadowed."

"Eunice Quelling-Steele," he said, "would give her right arm to look half as charming. Now will you tell me what Iris Goodfriend has got on? It looks like a couple of old altar cloths."

"It may well be. Peg says she's turning conservative."

This seemed to entertain Simon, and then the babble around them abruptly ceased as a door at the end of the gallery opened, and out filed half a dozen musicians bearing instruments. Taking their places on a raised platform, they commenced a preliminary sawing and tootling, until a bearded conductor emerged and briskly drew them to attention.

The music was sprightly but fairly repetitious, and Lucia began to look about her, contemplating first the barrel-vaulted ceiling and its honeycomb panelling, which acoustically speaking worked extremely well, and then the backs of heads (Dr. Jenna's, still as a carving, could be seen several rows ahead), and finally the conglomeration of Ravensmoor portraits hanging on the long wall opposite the windows.

In the sixteenth century they were all dark-eyed, these

bygone Ravensmoors, purse-mouthed as if their ruffs were too tight, pale and long-nosed like El Greco grandees; but by the eighteenth century they had grown less bilious and more robust and developed the rose-stained cheeks which Tony had inherited. It was in that century, too, that a merry red-headed lady with a wicked eye had entered the family, as manifested in a delightful likeness that stood out among the dark-haired strain, a lady who deposited red-headed genes which cropped up at intervals in successive generations. Some distance away Lucia made out a contemporary portrait of a heavy-set young man wearing a slate-blue uniform and huge World War II moustaches, flame-red; could this be the present Viscount, the expatriot high-living older brother of the Hon. Antony?

Lucia realized then that, having viewed this panorama of ancestors, she knew Antony Farr somewhat better. If he wasn't as chivalrous to bumbling Americans as he was to an overbearing Englishwoman who'd cost him twenty thousand pounds, the reason was there on the wall in the unwavering stares of a patrician breed removed from the common herd.

A burst of applause roused her. The first half of the concert was over and everyone rose for the interval, making for the buffet downstairs. Tony Farr, Lucia discovered, had been sitting behind her on the aisle, and was exchanging a word or two with his neighbors.

"You prefer ancestors," he remarked as she passed, "to early English composers."

Chagrined, she answered the first thing that came into her head: "I thought you listened to music with your eyes shut."

He actually broke into a full smile, almost a laugh. "Not if there's something," he said, "or someone, interesting to watch." And he disappeared into the crowd as Lady Quelling-Steele, with a glare for Lucia, approached.

In fact, Tony vanished for the rest of the evening. Lady

Quelling-Steele looked bored and furious, sipping champagne in the refreshment bar and barely acknowledging the salutations addressed to her. She surveyed Lucia in her simple dress with loathing, but she did manage a smile and a shrug for Simon. Rodney looked even more bored than she. They didn't return to their seats for the last half of the concert.

SIMON saw his aunts to their door and then walked Lucia to hers. He kissed her lightly on the lips and said, "I shall be sleeping only a few yards from you. That, I hope, is progress." And he left her, laughing once more.

Inside, with the door shut, she knew instantly that there was someone in the house.

Upstairs there was a faint, stealthy sound.

Like a shot, Lucia was outside again and running next door for help.

Adelaide's answer was to pick up a poker and storm over to Bloodrose House herself, followed by Simon and Lucia, remonstrating in vain.

They searched the house from top to bottom, in every nook and cranny. There was no one there. Nothing was disturbed.

Whoever it was, Lucia decided, heart still pounding, must have got out when she ran next door.

Simon and Adelaide thought she must have been mistaken, although they didn't quite say so. "Old houses are always making odd noises," declared Adelaide. But Simon, noting that Lucia still trembled, offered to change places with her—he sleeping in Bloodrose House while she slept in Adelaide's spare room.

"Capital!" cried Adelaide. "Come at once!"

There was no arguing with her, and in any case, Lucia was too shaken to refuse.

· *XIII* ·

IT was a morning of comings and goings at Blood-rose House. Simon removed himself early, so as not to startle Mrs. Berry when she arrived at nine, and Lucia returned from Adelaide's house.

She called Slade immediately and requested that her locks be changed. *"Today,"* she said unequivocally.

"May I ask why, Madam?"

"Because I think someone has a key to the front door," she said. "Someone, every now and then, is using it."

Next, heart thudding, she telephoned the Ravensmoor Arms. "Is Lady Quelling-Steele there?"

"No, Madam, she checked out early this morning."

So that was that. It was a relief, at least, that the woman had left town.

Then Simon, having bathed and breakfasted, returned to Bloodrose House to say goodbye. He was leaving that afternoon for Paris and a fortnight's business trip on the Continent. They took their coffee into the garden, out of the way of Mrs. Berry and her omniverous vacuum cleaner.

"Come with me," he said. "The change will do you good." Makeup didn't hide the fact that she was wan and hollow-eyed from the night before. "Come to Paris with me."

She smiled, shaking her head. "Lovely thought!"

"I'll try not to seduce you, if that's what's worrying you."

"Noble Simon."

"I wish for once you'd take me seriously."

She put out her hand and he grasped it. "Simon, I don't ever not take anyone seriously. I mean, I never don't take anyone seriously."

"Your writing, I trust, is not to be judged by your speech. All right, then, take this seriously." With his blue, half-humorous twinkle he looked into her eyes. "I'm in love with you, Lucia."

"Oh, Simon." Unthinkingly she withdrew her hand.

She'd been treating his regard for her as a flirtation, for his sake as well as hers, and probably she'd have done so without Adelaide's warning. He played the game himself. He delighted her, she was happy with him, there was even a dash of physical attraction in her fondness, and she wanted nothing to spoil an ideal—to her present way of thinking—relationship. She wasn't sure it would bear the weight of love. Love invited pain. Curiously, she was too fond of Simon to be in love with him.

"I know," he said. "I know you're getting over a bad time. I've kept that in mind. I know you're not ready for a full-blooded affair." Hands in pockets, ankles crossed, he stretched out comfortably in the rustic chair. "I don't want to bugger up what we have in the hope of something better. I shan't, as Charlotte would say, press my suit. But bear in mind that under my clown costume there beats a sober heart, and before your stay here is over I shall turn serious again." He gave her a grin.

She sat with her hands folded in her lap. She still couldn't quite believe him. She looked up at the roses climbing the sun-warmed wall of the house. She didn't know what possessed her; the question came out before she knew she was going to ask it. "Were you in love with Helen Farr?"

He gave her an astonished look. His color changed, blanching slightly and then reddening slightly, and his usually untroubled brow creased in a frown. "I may have thought so," he said, after a moment's consideration, as though deciding Lucia had a right to an answer. But there was an edge in his voice, a sharp edge Lucia had heard before, when he first spoke of Helen Farr.

She asked, "Could one be in love with her and not like her?"

He gave her another ambiguous answer. "A lot of people worshipped her. It wasn't hard for a woman as beautiful as Helen to turn people into slaves."

Lucia studied her clasped hands. "Well, Simon, this is probably sacrilege, but honestly, the more I hear about Helen Farr, the more she sounds detestable!"

Simon tipped back and looked into the branches overhead. She thought he was going to laugh, as Lady Quelling-Steele had done, the crushed laugh of irony, but in fact he gave vent to a little puff of a sigh. He closed his eyes for a second. He said finally, once more, "Come to Paris with me."

So he had changed the subject again, but she gave him credit for answering at all, even ambiguously. "Thank you, Simon, but no. *You* might not seduce me, but Paris might, and the result would be disastrous for us. Anyway, I couldn't come if I wanted to. My mother arrives soon and I must make some preparations."

Yet she hated to part with him. When he kissed her goodbye in the hall she wanted instinctively to put her arms around his neck and cling to him, and as he went down the steps to his car it ocurred to her, and not for the first time, that he might have come to mean more to her than she would let herself believe.

As Simon drove away, Dr. Jenna approached on his return from morning rounds. He stopped in front of his house, got out and reached for his medicine case. He then walked not into his own house but down the street, opposite Lucia, and into Miss Morgan's house.

Had Miss Morgan cracked at last under the strain of her own mania? She'd certainly seemed on the verge of a breakdown the last time Lucia had seen her, in the churchyard.

The accustomed manner with which Dr. Jenna let himself into Miss Morgan's house made Lucia wonder if he occasionally had to administer sedatives, or tranquilizers.

AROUND noon, soon after Mrs. Berry left, there was a peremptory rat-tat of the door-knocker, and Lucia, peeking warily out a parlor window, saw an old sports car with spindly wire wheels and its top down parked in front of the house. Slade must have reported her telephone call to his employer, for she opened the door to Antony Farr.

"What happened?" he said, without a greeting. "Are you all right?"

"Yes, I'm all right." Surprise immobilized her for a second or two, and then automatically she stepped back, opening the door wider, not quite inviting him to come in since she knew it was abhorrent to him but suggesting he was welcome and that in the interests of privacy it might be a good idea. And to her further surprise he gave her a sharp dark stare as though making up his mind and, tweed cap in hand, stepped over the threshold.

Again without words, not pressing the point, she raised a hand to indicate the parlor, but this time he gave her a curt shake of the head and remained standing just inside the door, which he'd closed behind him, not shifting his eyes from her face. He demanded once more, "What happened?"

Involuntarily her hand went to her throat as she found herself a little short of breath. After all, it was a rather momentous occasion, his setting foot in Bloodrose House for the first time, as far as she knew, since his wife died. And then, too, it was the first time they'd stood face to face, alone, the silent house shutting out the world, and his height, his vivid coloring, had something of a physical impact, one that alarmed her like the ominous rumble of thunder and that she didn't understand at all.

She took a breath and told him what had happened.

"I didn't mean to make a fuss," she finished, "but once before I thought someone had got into the house, although nothing was taken, and for my own peace of mind I asked Mr. Slade to change the locks. I'll pay for it if you feel—"

"Of course not."

When Antony Farr said "Of course not" in that tone, there could be no further discussion. And Lucia knew this would have rubbed her the wrong way at another time and place, even though it had been said in her favor; but here in Bloodrose House, incongruously, they were on neutral ground, and nothing one said to the other could be taken amiss. If he could surrender his phobia about the house, she could surrender her touchiness.

He asked, "Do you suspect someone?"

"Yes." The blunt question made her hesitate. "But I—I'm not sure—I'd hate to incriminate someone who—"

"Yes. All right, the locksmith will be along after lunch. Let's hope this takes care of the matter." He shook his crumpled cap at her, touching her bare forearm with it. "But I want you to promise me you'll let me know if there's any further trouble."

"I promise."

He took a step backwards and found the doorknob behind him. His face softened momentarily as his eyes met hers. "I've an idea you keep promises," he said. He opened the door, halted an instant to send a stunned stare around him at the white paint and the welter of roses in the sitting room, then gave Lucia a nod, and left.

SHE stood for several minutes without moving, after the putter of his two-seater had faded away. In no way had he suggested she might be imagining things.

Yet the fact that he believed her did nothing to lessen her fears; on the contrary, it made the unreal situation real. Had she hoped someone would convince her she *was* imagining things? Now she had to put a stop to emotional palpitations, muster up a calm fortitude she wasn't sure she was capable of, and come rationally to grips with the problem.

She might have got home from the concert sooner than she was expected. But if she'd got home when she *was* expected, if she hadn't heard the faint movement upstairs, what would have happened?

What sort of trap would she have walked into?

The rational approach didn't seem to calm her fears either.

·XIV·

FESTIVAL Week ended, and June slid into July. Farm machines had reached a peak of activity in the fields. The lambs of April were becoming sheep. Thistles bloomed and ox-eye daisies starred the grass. The rusty crown of Ravensmoor turned green.

The Fourth of July quietly came and went, and although Lucia was less apprehensive for her personal safety now that her locks had been changed, she felt claustrophobic and homeless. She didn't belong anywhere, she thought, and the fact that someone might *want* her to feel she didn't, shadowed her days.

There wasn't a sign of life across the street, and Lucia would have concluded Miss Morgan had gone away, except that one day, returning from market, she spied Dr. Jenna and Peg Goodfriend going into Miss Morgan's house together. If these two had joined forces, something was seriously wrong.

"Miss Morgan must be sick," Lucia said to Mrs. Berry while she put away her purchases.

Mrs. Berry was wringing out tea towels and hanging them up to dry. "Aye," she said. "Aye, she may be sick."

Lucia gave her a sharp sideways glance. "Do you know what's the matter with her?"

There was a slight pause as Mrs. Berry drained the sink. "She has spells," she said at last, polishing the stainless steel.

"Oh?" queried Lucia, an English upward-sliding Oh? meaning, Elucidate. Mrs. Berry folded her lips, but Lucia persisted: "Spells, Mrs. Berry?"

"Aye, spells," reiterated Mrs. Berry stubbornly. "There, now, I've finished and I'll be taking off. I'll bring you a marrow tomorrow, they're crawling all over my garden."

And while Lucia got sidetracked, picturing Mrs. Berry's marrows crawling about her garden, Mrs. Berry scuttled away.

But she had confirmed Lucia's belief that the people of Foxwold were keeping a lid on something.

LUCIA made yet another trip to Haworth, to walk the moors frequented by the Brontë sisters, and she took heart herself from Charlotte's courage. Charlotte, too, must have felt homeless and solitary in the silent parsonage, but had made a home within herself, in her own creative wellspring, and the deaths of her sisters one by one, Branwell's madness, her father's seclusion, and the forbidding countryside had not defeated her as they might have done anyone else.

NEVERTHELESS it was a relief, Lucia found, to drive down to York on the appointed day to meet the Aberdonian on its way from London to Scotland, and to spot her mother's small, trim, fastidious figure stepping out of a distant car. An obliging train conductor followed with her bags and hailed a porter for her.

Mrs. Fairburn wasn't by any means what could be called elderly, although her reddish-blonde hair had faded to a pale straw-color, but she was the kind of person to whom strangers spontaneously chatted or lent assistance. She was dressed in a knitted suit with little gold buttons, size six, not in beige or navy but a clear cardinal red; her feet were beautifully shod and she wore gloves, and anyone could see at a glance she was American, decent, and nobody's fool.

Lucia, no longer feeling displaced, shedding nebulous shadows, fear, and suspicions as she ran, hurried to greet her.

ONCE again Will Luddington plunged down his front steps to help with luggage, for Lucia's friends knew her mother was arriving today, and Lucia would never forget the look of rapture in his craggy face as he took the hand of a little lady who appeared to meet all his chivalrous standards.

"What a nice man," said Mrs. Fairburn in the front hall of Bloodrose House, after the Admiral had left them. "And there are the roses you wrote me about. Really, Lucia, it's charming!"

But Lucia held her breath as she conducted her mother up to the front bedroom. Her mother had her own infallible taste. Her apartment in Bronxville was furnished with treasures from the house that had been sold, most of them diminutive like herself, and set off by her favorite clear colors, coral or geranium or airy robin's egg blue. Therefore Lucia could hardly wait to hear her comment on Lady Quelling-Steele's romantic masterpiece.

But all she said was, "My goodness," in so quiet, polite, and astonished a manner that Lucia burst into laughter.

"Will you be all right here, Mother? Would you rather—?"

"I'll be perfectly comfortable." Mrs. Fairburn chuckled. "This is the kind of bedroom I dreamed of having when I was twelve!" And so saying she moved to the dressing table, put down her purse, removed her gloves, and began unbuttoning her jacket.

Lucia, going downstairs to fix lunch, found it whimsical that the ghost of Helen Bellington Farr was about to be exorcised, not by a pair of lustful lovers, but by dainty, sensible, collected Nancy Mills Fairburn of Bronxville, New York.

IF Lucia had worried that lights in the sacrosanct front bedroom might trigger a serenade of haunting cries under the window, her worries were groundless. The nights were as still as only those of a sleeping village in the country can be, and Mrs. Fairburn rested undisturbed.

Once again Lucia began to believe her troubles were over.

THE days passed pleasantly. Lucia and her mother went sightseeing, down to York Minster and Castle Howard or up into the dales and through choice villages, to the ruins of old abbeys and castles; picnicking sometimes or lunching in pubs and inns to which Lucia had been introduced by Simon. They took in Foxwold's weekly market and browsed in antique shops. Will Luddington wined and dined them at the Arms, the Goodfriends had them to tea, they lunched with the Ambrose sisters, and Simon returned from the Continent in time to take them, with the Admiral for a fourth, to a very splendid dinner at the Grand Hotel in Scarborough. Between times, Mrs. Fairburn read or worked on her needlepoint in the garden, and helped Lucia prepare appetizers for the party she was giving for her mother on Sunday.

On Saturday, after a night of thunderstorms, when the leftover clouds had evaporated and gardens glowed in the still, hot, morning sunshine, Peg Goodfriend called to say she was driving over to Farthing to pick some lilies for the church and would Lucia and her mother like to go along and lend a hand? Tony, who was leaving early for the Great

Yorkshire Agricultural Show in Harrogate, had invited her to help herself and told her to ask Gredge for anything she needed.

If they'd been alone when they pulled away from Bloodrose House, Lucia might have asked Peg what was the matter with Miss Morgan, but Peg was outlining the Ravensmoor family for Mrs. Fairburn, who sat next to her on the front seat, and Lucia decided she didn't want to talk about Miss Morgan anyway.

The great tawny house came into view as they went up the long drive, and Lucia again felt a lift of the heart at the sight of it. As if in a dream of returning to a childhood home, she felt a start of recognition, a gladness that anything so old and so beautiful could endure in so destructive a world, could go on standing in its own inviolate tranquility.

"Oh!" exclaimed Mrs. Fairburn softly.

"Yes, it's a gem, isn't it?" said Peg. "We're all thankful it's still lived in and cared for by one of the family. I expect we have Helen Farr and her chocolate factory to thank for that, really, but wherever the upkeep comes from, it's worth saving."

So Antony Farr *had* inherited from Helen, thought Lucia, with a sinking feeling. She'd hoped, for all their discord, that he was above suspicion.

But it was too lovely a morning for worrisome thoughts, and she resolutely set Tony Farr, as well as Miss Morgan, aside in her mind.

They drove up to the house and around it to the later seventeenth-century additions at the rear, stables and outbuildings of mellow brick, and Peg located Gredge in his greenhouse. With a slow arthritic hobble he conducted them around a terrace and down through a formal rose garden to a sunken square of lawn, enclosed by old brick walls and bordered by masses of pink lilies. Peg had brought containers and clippers, and when Gredge had shown them where to find water he cautioned, with a tear leaking down his ruddy cheek, "Mind t'bees," and left them.

They all three set to work.

In half an hour their containers were filled and they sat down for a moment, Peg and Mrs. Fairburn on a wooden bench and Lucia on the grass at their feet.

The sunny quiet, the heady scent of lilies, the hum of bees, were hypnotic. A dog barked from a distant farm, and somewhere in the shrubbery a blackbird warbled its pensive phrases.

"This garden must have been laid out when the house was built," said Mrs. Fairburn. "Do you suppose these are descendants of the original lilies?"

"Oh no," said Peg. "Helen Farr planted them."

Lucia groaned inwardly. Helen Farr was a tough ghost to exorcise; it seemed as if they were never free of her for long.

Arms folded, eyes squinting at an ancient sundial in the center of the lawn, Peg added, "She had the original Elizabethan garden torn out."

Mrs. Fairburn gave a little gasp. "What a shame!"

"Lord Ravensmoor was not pleased."

"You mean," exclaimed Lucia, turning to Peg, "she did it without his *permission?*" It didn't sound like the kind of thing Tony would consent to either.

"Helen Farr wasn't in the habit of asking permission," said Peg, with that familiar edge in her voice. "It was the beginning of the rift between them."

"Between Helen Farr and the Viscount?" Lucia was learning despite her inborn discretion to ask blunt questions, even if she didn't get answers. "What sort of rift?"

"One that ended with their being evicted."

"With who being evicted?" Her English really was getting sloppy, as Simon had pointed out.

"Tony and Helen. George had invited them to live at Farthing when they married, had a wing fixed up for them. Generous George; it was not a good idea. Or could it have

118

been Helen's idea? Anyway, there was some kind of row, finally—Tony would never breathe a word about it, and Helen only smiled charitably—and they moved out, to Bloodrose House, while George spent more and more time in the south of France." Peg made a dry twist of a smile. "As for the lilies, Helen won lots of prizes with them, and magnanimously gave them away, and here they still are." Peg unfolded her arms. "That's enough gossip from me. It was a long time ago. Shall we go back?"

But brisk footsteps were coming along behind the brick wall, and in the next instant Tony Farr appeared. He carried his jacket over his shoulder and his sleeves were rolled up.

"Hello, Peg," he began, descending the steps into the garden, "I hoped I'd get back before you—" He broke stride at sight of Lucia and Mrs. Fairburn. "Oh, good morning." He came forward, throwing his jacket over his arm to free his hand.

Lucia introduced her mother, and Mrs. Fairburn looked up into the tall man's face and smiled, and Tony Farr, although not seized with a fit of gallantry like Will Luddington, brought his heels together and took her hand and bowed easily from the waist. "I heard you were at Bloodrose House," he said. "I hope you're enjoying Yorkshire."

"I am indeed." Mrs. Fairburn seldom said anything that was untrue or unnecessary.

"We were just leaving," said Peg. "I must get back to fix Cedric's lunch. Thanks for the lilies. The Flower Committee will be so pleased."

"Don't go," he said, perhaps a little more abruptly than he intended, for his face underwent that suggestion of metamorphosis, a subcutaneous ripple, from sternness and distance to possibilities of good humor. His coloring had deepened, the skin tanned by the sun in the days since Festival Week. "Come up to the house. Mrs. Clay keeps cold lemonade on hand for me in this hot weather; would you like a glass? Gredge will put your flowers in your car."

They agreed and strolled back to the terrace. Bless Peg, thought Lucia, half-enviously. She was never uneasy with anyone, or they with her.

Tony took them inside and guided them into a darkly paneled room, not one of the great rooms but one which had the lived-in look of a favorite lair. He said to Mrs. Fairburn, "If you had more time I'd show you about. Please sit down, and I'll go and find Mrs. Clay and speak to Gredge."

They seated themselves in worn leather chairs and a sofa and waited in relaxed silence. It was cool in the room, lighted from casement windows open to the rose garden, and it smelled of wood ashes in the hearth, which hadn't been emptied in a long time, probably by Tony's orders, for the rest of the room was well dusted and polished. Farming and sporting magazines were neatly stacked on a table, there was a flat desk with a telephone, and the walls were crowded with eighteenth-century portraits of horses with wild lustrous eyes, attended by grooms, and glowing paintings of fruit and game birds. A typical English gentleman's study.

But no portrait, no photograph, of his dead wife.

One couldn't exactly feel sorry for a man at home in such a handsome room, but Lucia detected the faint underlying taint of affliction, like the smell of ashes; the duress of solitude, perhaps, so familiar and habitual that the man might not even be aware of it himself anymore.

Mrs. Clay, a stout gray-haired Scotswoman, brought a tray of glasses and a pitcher of lemonade with sprigs of mint in it, and right away fell into friendly conversation with Peg, inquiring after her health and that of the rector and the lass, Miss Iris. This was surely the woman who had blocked and dried her hat, thought Lucia. Peg introduced her and her mother, and Mrs. Clay declared it was a pleasure to meet Mrs. Vail at last, and wasn't Fairburn a Scottish name? It was, said Lucia's mother, and they conferred about this until Tony returned, when Mrs. Clay wished them a good morning and withdrew.

While they sipped their lemonade, Peg questioned Tony about the Great Yorkshire Show, and they discussed beef champions and heavy horses and other categories, until Tony broke off, apologizing to Mrs. Fairburn for talking shop.

"I enjoy listening to people who know what they're talking about," she said, adding with a little smile, "even if *I* don't."

He gave her a little glimmer of approval. He turned to Lucia, but she was gazing out the casement window. She'd been wearing a broad-brimmed straw hat which she'd pulled off, and in a flowered cotton dress she was a picture of summer repose. If he'd been about to say something he let it go, and contemplated her.

She became aware of a silence and came out of her trance to meet dark and unfathomable eyes. "I'm not bored either," she told him, "but Farthing has a lulling effect this morning."

"A lulling effect," he echoed, sampling the words, as if trying to imagine such a thing. "Yes," he murmured, without taking his eyes from hers. "Perhaps it has."

There was another silence, then Peg got to her feet and said she really must be off, and they filed out onto the terrace again and strolled around toward the back of the house, Peg and Mrs. Fairburn chatting in front and Lucia and Tony uncommunicative behind.

He spoke before they left the shade of the house. "You too," he said quietly, "have a lulling effect. You're not really a contentious person at all, are you?"

Surprised, she shook her head. "No, I'm really not."

"More healing than hurting. More ruthful than ruthless."

Too startled to reply, not knowing whether he was reciting something or actually putting thoughts into words, she looked up at him, and he gave her a little ironic smile, as if to say he'd surprised himself; as if to say, I'm not entirely unfeeling, you see.

They rounded the house and approached Peg's estate

wagon. Peg thanked him once more, Mrs. Fairburn gave him her hand, and they got into the front seat together.

Lucia grasped the handle of the rear door, but said before opening it, "I hope you're coming to my party for my mother tomorrow." She'd sent him an invitation but hadn't received an answer.

He stiffened. This was a setback. Teeth on edge, eyes lowered, he wrestled with private distress. She almost put out her hand to say, Never mind, don't come, it doesn't matter.

But it did matter, somehow; it was ridiculous and important at the same time, and she waited for his response.

He exhaled a little sigh, the only sign of what this cost him. "All right," he said, staring at her in alarm. And then he reached out and grasped her wrist as if in a desperate pledge. "For you, all right." He let go of her wrist immediately.

She opened the door and climbed into the rear seat. He closed the door after her, turned on his heel, and strode away, hands in pockets, hunched over.

Swamped in the scent of lilies Gredge had stowed behind the rear seat, Lucia wondered if she'd made a terrible mistake. Had she really done him a favor? Or done herself one?

As they left Farthing and headed up the rise of Ravensmoor she felt as though, having pushed Antony Farr across a Rubicon, she'd ventured into dangerous territory as well, where she had no business being, and from which there might not be an easy way or any way back at all.

·XV·

THE weather was still fine on Sunday, warm but with no threat of a late-afternoon shower.

The Reverend Goodfriend delivered that morning a rousing sermon on the devil, a favorite with his congregation. If one could accept the existence of a force for good, he reasoned, then it oughtn't to be impossible to accept a force for evil, and his recognition of Satan, backed by resounding chapter and verse, never failed to hold his parishioners' attention.

"The devil is come down unto you, having great wrath, because he knoweth he hath but a short time!"

It reminded Lucia uncomfortably of "Get out, before it's too late!" She didn't find it at all difficult to accept a force for evil.

Her mother beside her, gloved hands folded, was perfectly composed as usual, listening attentively. Lucia looked down at her own clenched hands and made herself unclasp them.

Right in front of Lucia sat the Ambrose sisters, Olivia's white hair looking like the spun glass of which Christmas tree angels were made, and Adelaide with her shoulders squared, staunchly anti-Satan. In Adelaide's school there was no such thing as a hopeless student or an evil child. Adelaide, ever in the here and now, shunned the abstract; Olivia had always had one foot in heaven.

Will Luddington, across the aisle, scowled, beetle-browed. He, too, defied the force of evil. He might be guilty of letting people think he was an admiral, thought Lucia, but surely the devil would consider this slim pickings.

Directly in front of him in a straw hat trimmed with poppies sat Peg Goodfriend, with Iris, whose tender neck was revealed under a new hairdo, her frizzy silken mop piled every which way on top of her head. What did Peg think of Cedric's sermon, Lucia wondered, knowing Peg had few illusions about the way of the world. Nor could Lucia really believe Peg had ever done anything wicked enough to warrant a guilty conscience. Her tears of distress over Helen Farr must have emanated from her own goodness. And Iris? But Iris had a kind of shameless innocence which the devil would find it very hard to infiltrate.

A few rows ahead, in the pew traditionally reserved for members of the Ravensmoor family, sat Antony Farr, arms folded, head thoughtfully inclined. It was impossible to tell whether the sermon was making him uncomfortable or whether he was thinking about champion beef.

Beyond his head, on and about the altar, Helen Farr's prize lilies were massed, their scent faintly permeating the air. Waxen, trembling, open-mouthed like trumpets, they struck Lucia as somehow obscene. While Cedric rounded out his sermon, calling on his congregation to turn to the True Light, which lighteth every man and woman that cometh into the world, the lilies, as if sweetly cynical, looking on from some skeptical, unearthly plane, seemed to mock him.

And then Lucia's overworked senses told her that while she watched those in front of her, someone behind watched her.

A little ripple of gooseflesh ran up the back of her neck. She turned her head quickly before she could stop herself, and met the gleaming eyes of Miss Morgan.

Lucia faced forward again immediately, while the eyes behind her, she felt, still pierced the back of her neck.

"Be sober," thundered Cedric, "be vigilant; because your adversary, the devil, as a roaring lion, walketh about, seeking whom he may devour!"

Then briskly he came down from the pulpit, the congregation roused itself with a little rustle, and the organ burst forth in clarion notes.

There was a sickness in Miss Morgan's face, Lucia brooded as she joined in the closing hymn, that hadn't been there before. Even in that brief backward glance Lucia had noticed the reddened lids and purpled cheeks, the porous and puffy skin, the glazed eyes. Once more Lucia felt if it hadn't been for the malevolence directed at her she could have pitied the woman.

Lucia had no desire to meet those unhappy eyes again. When the service ended, she turned to speak to Adelaide and Olivia, delaying their exit, and by the time she turned and filed down the aisle after her mother, Miss Morgan was nowhere in sight.

EVERYONE was curious about the kind of party a resident American would give, everyone was interested in Lucia's small, attractive mother, everyone wanted to see what Lady Quelling-Steele had done to Bloodrose House; consequently everyone who had been invited came to the party, including those who knew Lucia only casually.

The house was filled with roses, and the garden was at its best. It was Mrs. Fairburn's idea to set several small tables and chairs out on the lawn, covering the tables with pink sheets from Woolworth's and decorating them with roses and votive candles stuck in brandy goblets. A bar was set up handy to the kitchen door, with a hired bartender, and a table at the opposite end of the garden, lighted also with makeshift hurricane lamps, was laden with food.

As a final touch, Lucia with Iris's help had tracked down a pair of young musicians who played the flute and a harp and sang gentle folk airs. They stationed themselves at the far end of the garden, near the door to the lane, rather arty in their Olde English costumes, the girl with a wreath of flowers over her long hair and the youth with a bushy red beard, but fresh and pleasant-sounding in the open air and not objectionably loud.

"Foxwold has never seen anything like it," Simon told Lucia.

"It's not too showy, I hope." Besides honoring her mother Lucia wanted also to say thank you to her Foxwold friends.

"It is not. It befits you. As does your white frock—demure yet desirable. I want to follow you about the way Will Luddington follows your mother. Your mother, I might add, holds Foxwold in the palm of her hand."

They looked across the grass at her, surrounded by well-wishers, with the Admiral hovering nearby.

"She's a winner!" pronounced Mrs. O'Bailey, muscular in bare-shouldered black, as she passed Lucia and Simon. "Might almost be English!"

Simon gave Lucia an owlish wink, and she smothered a laugh. Iris, they noted, was wearing altar-cloths again, her hair still half-pinned up, or half-falling down.

Antony Farr arrived.

He stopped on the study steps, and his rigid mask dissolved into bewilderment. The garden with its lights and music, the high babble of voices, combined to make a sort of fiesta, and he looked nonplussed, shocked perhaps, to find gaiety where there had been grief.

Heads turned and smiles broke out, and the party suddenly became a celebration.

Lucia went to Tony at once. "Welcome," she said simply. His eyes swung about to her and she saw consternation in them, as if he might turn and run. "I'm so glad you've come." He didn't or couldn't say a word. "Come over to the bar for a drink."

He let her lead him to the bar, and then she steered him to

her mother, whose stabilizing effect immediately went to work on him, and very quickly he seemed to recover himself.

The dreaded moment was over.

In fact he seemed to enjoy himself, circulating about, prominent with his long-limbed height and look of breeding. An endangered species, thought Lucia. That kind of breeding was called elitism in the States and frowned upon, and she suspected it might be on its way out in Britain as well.

When it began to grow dark and the moment came when people thought of leaving, he sought her out. "Thank you," he said rather formally, "for persuading me to come."

And rather than seek the egotism in this as she might once have done, she could now take it at face value and find the exact opposite, and her eyes smarted. If he had been an American or a Simon Myles she would have stepped forward and given him a reassuring hug. But because he was on edge again, honourable and unfathomable, with a sorrow or a guilt so great that a hug would seem tasteless, if not cruelly lighthearted, she replied a little hoarsely, "It was time, probably."

"Yes," he agreed with gravity. He looked straight into her eyes. "But I wouldn't have come for anyone else."

Lucia never knew what her answer would have been.

For at that moment Miss Morgan appeared like a bedraggled fury on the study steps.

The front door had been left open for arriving and departing guests, and she had walked in.

"Get out!" she yelled at the gathering, wild-eyed, her dead-black hair disarranged, waving her arms, lurching to keep her balance. Everyone froze. "Get out of her garden! Who do you think you are, amusing yourselves in her house!"

Tony moved to her like lightning.

"And you!" she screamed. "Who'd have thought *you*

would turn traitor, making up to that bitch, that interloper!"

Dr. Jenna followed on Tony's heels, and Peg Goodfriend closed in from another quarter. Between them they got hold of her arms and wheeled her about.

"No!" she wailed, struggling. "She told me to keep watch! She said no one was to be happy here, ever again—!"

They rushed her away, so quickly that guests at the far end of the garden hardly knew what had happened. The Admiral had taken up a guardian stance at Mrs. Fairburn's side, and Simon went to Lucia, who was almost as white as her dress. She knew now what was meant by "spells."

"What a party!" said Simon. "As if Tony's turning up weren't sensation enough, we then have a cameo appearance from Miss Morgan! What next, love?"

She giggled, a trifle hysterically. Everyone else was bravely carrying on, winding up conversations where they'd left off and preparing to leave. "Bless you, Simon. I'll get back on the job."

She was in the front hall seeing off the last of her guests, save for Simon and his aunts and Will, who remained behind in the garden, when Tony returned from across the street.

"Jenna and Peg Goodfriend have taken her down to hospital in York," he told Lucia. "Jenna says she's been working up to this over the past few weeks. She can be charged with disturbing the peace and unlawful entry, but invariably after a month's treatment at Bootham she comes back docile as a lamb and behaves herself for a long time. I'll go down to York and talk to her when she's sobered up and give her warning. There's to be no more of this. She was attached to my late wife for many years; Helen bought the house across the street for her and left her a trust to provide for her needs. Unfortunately it provides as well for periodic bouts with the bottle. Lucia, I'm deeply sorry."

Indeed, he looked so sorry that she felt she must cheer him up. Once again they were alone in her hall. "Cedric's sermon this morning didn't do her a bit of good, did it?"

His tense dark face gave way to a smile. "Not in the way he intended." And once again he reached for her wrist, then slid her hand into his. "Lucia," he began, and stopped, and to her dismay his smile was replaced with a look of utter hopelessness. He looked down at her hand in his, as though bemused to see it there. "Lucia," he began again, and finished. He released her hand, gave her a last dark and harrowed look, said, "Good night," and went away.

Simon came in from the garden to find her standing alone at the door. "Come," he said softly. "Everything is picked up and shipshape, thanks to our efficient Admiral. The bartender is washing up, the minstrels await your dismissal, and we are about to have a post-party supper under the tree. Darling, it's time you sat down, you look all in."

Thankfully she took his arm, and they went outside.

·XVI·

"It's been a lovely week," said Mrs. Fairburn to Lucia over her needlepoint the following afternoon. "I really hate to leave."

They were sitting opposite each other by the sitting room fire. A soft rain in the night had developed into a squall in the daytime. Outside, branches thrashed, leaves and twigs flew through the air, and rain pelted the windows in gusts.

"You could marry Will Luddington," teased Lucia, "and

stay here for good." She had gathered together her boring, long-postponed sewing jobs and was shortening a hem, tightening loose buttons, and so on.

"Will Luddington is not about to ask anyone to marry him," replied Mrs. Fairburn, stitching serenely on. "He has a romantic nature and he likes yearning over someone, but the only way I could get him to marry me would be to ask him myself. He's too chivalrous to refuse!"

"So ask him," said Lucia, and thought probably the same measure would have to be taken with Simon, should someone wish to corner him.

"No," her mother told her. "I have a pleasant, peaceful life, and I'm not up to making drastic changes any more. Neither, I'm sure, is Will."

"Well, if you really hate to leave, how about staying with me until my lease is up, the end of September?"

Her mother looked up with a smile. "That's generous of you, dear. But I've made plans with Molly that I can't undo." She resumed her stitching. She knew, and Lucia knew she knew, that Lucia was ready to be alone again and get back to work. The fire snapped and hissed. "You seem to have got over the hump," said Mrs. Fairburn, "where Julian is concerned."

"Julian? Who's Julian?"

Her mother gave her bubbly laugh.

"No, seriously," said Lucia, "I don't dwell on him anymore. There are longer and longer periods when I don't even think of him. I'm putting him behind me and wanting to leave him there. I hope he's happy, and that's progress. For a long time I hoped he was miserable, like me!"

"I expect he's as happy as he knows how to be," said her mother. "They're having a baby, you know."

"No." The last pang. "I didn't know." Somewhere within her she shed the last tear—that it wasn't her baby, that he hadn't let her have one, that now it was over, really over.

"Surprisingly enough," said Mrs. Fairburn, "he telephones me now and then."

"Not surprising at all. He always admired and trusted you, men always do. Simon thinks you're perfection." Smoothly Lucia worked the conversation away from Julian. She never wanted to discuss him again; she had no more need of his name. She wanted no more of the past, she suddenly realized, as though the last thread binding her to it had been cut. She was tired of it; she knew that the present, for all its anxiety, was better.

A lingering past, she was learning, was like a lingering illness.

"Simon is extremely nice," her mother said, "and of course he adores you." She left it to Lucia to carry on from there. Not only did she seldom say anything unnecessary; she seldom said anything she didn't intend to say.

"Mmm," said Lucia, removing pins from a hem. "One hesitates to take advantage of him. I'm told he loves being in love."

"There are worse faults than that, aren't there? At any rate, I'm glad you've made such delightful friends, Simon included." Mrs. Fairburn rethreaded her needle. "And what about Tony Farr?"

Without moving a muscle Lucia started inwardly, becoming alert, on guard, at a standstill. "What about him?"

"Is he in love with you too?"

"Oh, my goodness, mother, no." Hotly making up for lost time, her pulse started up again, pumping heavily.

Mrs. Fairburn was silent. The wind flung rain across the windows. "There's something tragic about him, isn't there?" she said presently. "He's almost like a man with a secret illness."

The disease of the past, thought Lucia.

"Whatever it is," continued Mrs. Fairburn, "I hope he gets over it, for his sake as much as anyone else's."

"I hope so, too," Lucia agreed, her mother's warning

duly noted and accepted. But what had she taken in, this astute little woman, that Lucia had not, to ask that astounding question?

Lucia liked the subject of Antony Farr even less than that of Julian. Tony's name never came up, he never appeared in person, without causing her this perturbed start, this alarmed recoil, without making her feel at cross-purposes within herself.

"Well," said Mrs. Fairburn, "you must keep me posted on everyone, including that poor woman who lives across the street."

"I shall. It's odd, you know. I left Bronxville years ago, certainly I don't belong there any more, and New York doesn't appeal to me as it did when I was younger. But this," she gestured with one hand, "Foxwold, feels like home! In fact, I'm the one who hates to leave!" She added, after a moment's thought, "But I suppose when you learn to put the past behind you, you have to learn at the same time to face the future."

"There's another alternative," said her mother.

"Is there? What?"

"Enjoy the present moment, and let the future take care of itself."

"Will Luddington's motto! Simon's too!"

"Make it yours." Mrs. Fairburn looked up with a smile. "Is it too early for a cup of tea?"

A WEEK ago, before meeting her mother's train, Lucia had left some things to be dry-cleaned at a shop in York recommended by Peg Goodfriend, and after seeing her mother off to London, Lucia headed for the shop again to pick up her garments.

It was a wet afternoon, but the city was crowded, and Lucia had to park on a distant side street. It was when she left her car that she saw on the corner a street-sign saying South Gate.

Ellerbee & Son, 22 South Gate, York. The words flashed across the screen of her brain like a computer print-out. They headed the bills in the false bottom of the drawer in her desk at Bloodrose House.

Without decision, without thinking, she turned and followed the numbers down to 22.

There it was: Ellerbee & Son, Upstairs. It was a black plastic plate with white lettering, attached to the brick of the old building, and there was still nothing to specify whether it was a firm of solicitors or auctioneers or what.

In the next moment she found herself going up the wooden stairs, not knowing what she was going to do or say, but, even though in a slight flutter like a guilty eavesdropper, compelled to satisfy her curiosity.

As it turned out, she didn't have to go beyond the door. It contained an opaque glass pane on which was printed once more in dingy gold letters the name of father and son, but here at last they evidently felt it expedient to reveal the nature of their business, for in smaller gold letters in the lower lefthand corner of the pane were the words, Enquiry Agents.

Lucia had read enough British mystery stories to know that Enquiry Agents meant Private Detectives.

There wasn't a sound. The stillness was one of vacancy, but the feeling Lucia got from it was of someone lying in wait, beyond the door, watching and listening. There was a musty, faintly putrescent odor in the hall.

Hurriedly she turned and went down the stairs as though escaping from a trap, and out onto the street.

Taking a deep breath of fresh air, she resumed her walk to the dry-cleaners.

SHE wasn't sure she could open the compartment in the drawer again, but on her return to Bloodrose House she went straight to the desk and after repeated tries, again as if by accident, the molding dropped.

The bills from Ellerbee & Son had started coming to Helen Farr in the mid-1970s. There were eleven in all, spread over the years before her death, and Lucia added them up roughly to several thousand pounds.

Lucia returned them to the drawer and closed the molding, then sat for a while with her elbow on the desk and her chin in her hand. What had Helen Farr paid out so much money for, and why had she hidden the receipted bills? Did Tony know anything about them?

What had she been trying to find out?

·XVII·

THE wet weather continued right into August, and farmers grumbled.

Lucia was glad to have work to do indoors. Her book was nearly finished. There were a couple of chapters to pull together, after which she would sit down in an easy chair for a final read-through. This usually winnowed out a few pages to retype, and then the manuscript would go off to New York and she would have September, her last month at Bloodrose House, to do with as she pleased.

She was trying to follow her mother's suggestion to make the most of the present, but she did count on revisiting some of her favorite haunts before she had to say goodbye to Yorkshire. Perhaps one of the basic requirements for enjoying the present was to have something agreeable in the future to look forward to.

While the house across the street was dark and empty,

Lucia discovered in herself a lessening of tension. She hadn't realized how insidiously that watchful, jealous presence had worn her nerves until now when she was temporarily rid of it. With this freedom, and the confining, pacifying rain, she was capable of a prodigious amount of work.

She made the most of it. Miss Morgan would return. It wasn't petty warfare the woman waged, Lucia now knew, but a crusade. Lucia hadn't disregarded her drunken cries. It might be hard to believe that anyone, dying, would charge another with putting a curse, to speak, on her deathplace, but there was no doubt that Miss Morgan believed it. Lucia only hoped Miss Morgan sober was going to be an improvement over Miss Morgan drunk.

So while the month's respite lasted, while the rain spattered on the garden doors and the coal fire burned cozily, Lucia kept her nose to the typewriter.

By the end of the day she wasn't up to matching wits with anyone, especially not up to the sort of sexual fencing one engaged in with blithe Simon, and once again she begged for time. "Only a week or two more," she promised over the phone, "and I'll be ready for a fling."

"The longer you put me off, you know, the more dangerous I become."

"You're dangerous enough already, Simon." This was the kind of fencing she wasn't up to.

"Not dangerous enough to compete with Charlotte," he said, and Lucia could all but see his quizzical smile.

She made a final trip to the Brontë museum to check on a number of details, took her solitary walks over the fells behind Bloodrose House, and went up to the square to do her marketing. Otherwise she lived in a writer's limbo.

One afternoon, as she was returning from the post office, Iris Goodfriend popped out onto the rectory porch and hailed her. "Oh, Mrs. Vail, you're just the person we want to see! Please, please come in a minute!"

Lucia at once crossed the street to the rectory.

"Forgive us for waylaying you," said Peg, coming forward as Iris hung up Lucia's raincoat, "but we're in a quandary. We'd just decided you were the one to solve it for us when there you were, rounding the church." They ushered her into their snuggery, smaller than the formal rectory drawing room, a place where they could scatter magazines and sewing or curl up in a window seat with a book.

The quandary, it turned out, was a gown for Iris for the Harvest Ball at Farthing, on the last night of September.

"You'll be going yourself, of course," said Peg to Lucia. "It's *the* social event of the year." She rolled her eyes in mock-wonder. "Democratic Tony cuts across all classes, so don't be surprised at us: Everyone starts planning for it weeks, if not months, ahead."

"God," groaned Iris, "life in the country! Last year everyone *studiously* averted their eyes from my dress. Well, it wasn't really a dress, you know, just something I put together. And the year before that I was too young to be invited. This year I would like to look—to look—" Iris suddenly floundered.

"Beautiful," suggested Lucia.

Iris colored. "Oh, well, not beautiful, of course, but different, you know, civilized, maybe, or more like, like—"

"Like Lucia Vail," supplied Peg with a smile.

"But the problem is," Iris hurried on, blushing furiously, "do I make it or buy it or what? We can't afford a really *good* ball gown, but I *can* sew, you know, Mum taught me, I'm quite handy with a sewing machine. But what do I start out with? What sort of material, or pattern? Or rather, what do I want to end up with? If you could—if you would—help me choose?"

Lucia studied the pretty girl with the unmade hair, the green tights and purple leg-warmers under a red hip-length tunic, and thought Hmmm. She was very fond of her and had always wanted to see the real Iris in full bloom, uncamouflaged.

"Certainly I'll help." She couldn't attend to it right away, she told them, but if they didn't mind waiting a week or so she'd devote herself to the matter, and they thanked her enthusiastically.

"That's the ball Helen Farr started, isn't it?" she asked, getting into her raincoat again, having declined an invitation to tea.

They replied yes, it was, she did.

"While she was living at Farthing?"

"Just so."

"And Tony keeps it up?"

Peg nodded. "It was one of the nice things she did, that everyone enjoyed and made her so well-liked." And there was the guarded tone, the edgy tone, that came into Peg Goodfriend's voice, along with the fierce misery in her eyes, whenever she spoke of Helen Farr.

It was like putting together a difficult jig-saw puzzle, thought Lucia, as she splashed down the street to Bloodrose House in her rubber boots. Here were pieces of the saintly and well-loved Helen Farr, and there of the Helen Farr who wasn't in the habit of asking permission, who was always Number One, who left money to a dependent with an injunction to keep watch on the house where she'd died lest anyone presume to be happy in it; who hired private detectives over a number of years. . .

The filling out of this puzzle went on continuously now in the back of Lucia's mind, but the whole refused to emerge.

As for Tony Farr, her mind avoided him, walked around him as one would avoid a pasture harboring a dangerous animal. There were some people whom instinct told her it would be good to know better, and others she knew it would be best to give a wide berth.

"What, Iris Goodfriend?" cried Simon on the telephone

that night. "She's a sweet kid, certainly, but can you really see her in a ball gown? Could she carry it off?"

"She could if she thought she looked beautiful."

"Beautiful? Well, I know from the change you've wrought in me that you're capable of working miracles, but—"

"What change have I wrought in you, for heaven's sake?"

"You've made a monk of me. Full of prayer and meditation. Celibate above all."

"Idiot! Simon, take that pale, fine hair, the fine skin, the dimples, the tidy bosom: what do they suggest to you?"

"Forbidden territory for monks. What do they suggest to you?"

"Gainsborough."

It was his turn to laugh.

"Simon, be serious. Picture her in a dress of light-blue satin, a tiny waist, a sash that ties in back—"

"Darling, it's not a costume party, you know."

"It's not a costume I have in mind. She's had enough of costumes. I'm trying to work out a shape, a style, that would make the most of her. But I need your help. Where do I find material like that in Yorkshire? Where would I find a good selection of patterns?"

"There's always Marks & Spencer. If need be I could have some samples sent up from London. What about a hairdresser? When one thinks of Gainsborough one thinks of ringlets and tendrils, and when one thinks of Iris one thinks of an excruciating thatch. I say, you don't mind my getting into the act, do you? After all, I'm something of a Gainsborough expert."

"I hoped you *would* get into the act."

"Good. I warm to the idea. Tell you what, let's look at some pictures. I'll bring you one or two Gainsborough books."

"Wonderful. In a week or two."

He sighed. "Back to monkhood. All right, darling. Patience I'm learning also, along with obedience and celibacy."

THE sun came out at last, and farmers made up for lost time, their faces as they hurried in and out of the bank on the square showing the strain of hard-pressed labor.

Lucia had acquired a drawn look too. In the final coming-down-the-homestretch stage of finishing a book she was on tenterhooks lest something deflect her from the goal in sight, and only strung-out nerves kept complete exhaustion at bay.

"Takes it out of you, doesn't it?" called Adelaide, going indoors one morning as Lucia came out. "More power to you! See you when it's all over!" She closed her door, and Lucia, combining a necessary trip to the bank with a stop at the weekly market, hurried up the street.

The teller could have counted out five hundred pounds instead of fifty and she wouldn't have noticed. Even the familiar voice and figure of the farmer doing business at the next window failed to register in her preoccupied brain.

On the pavement outside he touched her shoulder. "Good morning, Lucia."

She wheeled and stared. "Oh. Tony. Good morning." Disoriented, shaken out of her preoccupation, she couldn't think of anything more to say.

He too stood rooted to the spot but as if making up his mind to something, the sun shadowing his eyes.

An extraordinary panic seized her. She took a step backward, preparing to flee before he came to whatever decision he was making. In the next instant he might utter something to put her on the spot, even something as innocuous as an invitation to coffee; even that might change the course of events beyond recall.

"It's a lovely day, isn't it?" she said, backing away. "I'm glad for the harvesters!" Did they use such a word in Yorkshire, or anywhere? She gave him a bright friendly smile, deliberately blurring her eyes to his expression. "Goodbye, I must run!" She turned, heart thumping, breath shortened, and without actually breaking into a run, paced with long strides down the street until there was an opening in traffic and she could cross into the market.

She didn't look back.

The absurd, the indecent thing was that as she worked her way through the market throng to the fruit stall, tears filled her eyes.

An arm slipped through hers as she completed her purchases. "Come into the Snack Bar and have a cake with me."

With a gasp and another explosive leap of the heart she wheeled. False alarm; it was Cedric Goodfriend.

"Oh, I'm sorry, Cedric, but I—"

"Come." On his free arm hung a laden basket. "We could both use a sugar-boost."

Had he spotted her distress of a few minutes ago, the momentary filling of the eyes? He was putting on a restrained version of his wobbly, absent-minded act, but his hand was firm under her arm, urging her along with him.

She gave him a resigned grin. "All right. I love cake before lunch."

She had spent nearly six months getting to know her neighbors, and they had a hold on her now that couldn't be broken. She might turn and run from one of them, only to be taken in charge by another. Even doing Iris over, if not an out-and-out ego-trip, was a responsibility about which she ought to have second thoughts. But she had a fatalistic feeling that no matter how hard she tried to resist, she was being drawn willy-nilly into that unknown course of events.

A booth was just emptying in the crowded Snack Bar. They slid into it and ordered, and Cedric removed his glasses and rubbed his eyes.

She said at once, commiseratively, "Summer is wearying for pastors, isn't it, as well as farmers?"

"And for writers."

So he *had* noticed. "Harvest-time for me, too, is near at hand."

"Splendid. We must enjoy life, you know; it's part of our obligation to our Creator." The girl brought their coffee and cake. "Peg's the tireless one," continued Cedric. "At this moment she's helping the young Crowders move into their new cottage, which means she'll fetch and carry, feed and change the baby, sweep up a bit and wash out a few things, and be home to get our lunch at one."

"It exhausts me just to hear about it!" In fact, if it had been anyone but Peg, one might have wondered if she were running from something.

"Energy!" Cedric waved his long arms like a wind-mill. "Genes! Metabolism!"

"And she won't say a word about her kindness to anyone."

"What's more to the point," rejoined Cedric, "she won't say a word about it to herself."

Thoughtfully Lucia stirred her coffee. "The small unsung good deeds, like changing someone's baby and sweeping up a bit, have so much more goodness, haven't they, than the big splashy ones, like starting a music festival or inaugurating a charity ball—the sort of thing that ensures the benefactor a lot of public credit?"

Cedric shot her a sharp, disquieted glance. Nervously he wiped the crumbs from his lips with a paper napkin. "They have their place also, Lucia, in the scheme of things."

"Yes, but . . ." She was really thinking out loud, trying to clarify a half-realized perception, completing another little part of the jigsaw puzzle. "But there's something sinister about someone who makes people feel guilty if they don't admire her, don't you think?"

He goggled at her, yet not as if he didn't understand her contorted question. He actually looked a little gray in the face. He hoisted a shoulder and scrabbled in his pocket for pence. "I must run. I think I shall make lunch for Peg for a change, and try not to tell myself about it."

Outside on the doorsill of the shop Lucia detained him. "I'm sorry. I didn't mean to speak ill of the dead."

He stood squinting out at the busy market stalls. "We must look," he said, almost in a whisper, so that Lucia had to lean closer to hear him over the drone of the market, "we must look at the sad and desperate need to achieve superiority . . . rather than at the inferior means used to achieve it." Lucia was pondering this when he added, "She had an incredible talent, a positive genius, for finding out how to persuade people . . . to do her bidding." Cedric turned and gave Lucia a stare of such cynicism and bitterness that it was hard to believe it came from a servant of God.

But Cedric, Lucia reminded herself, believed in the Devil.

He bade her good morning, stepped down to the street and set off, coattails flapping, in the direction of the rectory.

Helen Farr had succeeded in making even Cedric Goodfriend feel guilty.

And Lucia thought she had a clue now, however obscure, to the bills from Ellerbee & Son.

The person she would like to have run across, but didn't, was Dr. Jenna. It was a busy time for doctors, evidently, as well as farmers, clergymen, and writers. Every afternoon the cars lined up outside his surgery.

She considered making an appointment to see him about the crick in her neck, which she knew from experience would disappear as soon as she finished her book. There were a lot of questions she would have liked to ask him. For one, how Miss Morgan was doing and when she would be coming home. Tony had mentioned that Miss Morgan had in the past come home much improved after a month at Bootham. It was already three weeks since the party.

But although Dr. Jenna had been in his way almost affable at the party, in his office he was quite another character, and she would get nowhere.

A familiar uneasiness, a sense of foreboding, began to creep back into her outlook. Or was it the ever-nearing grief of leaving what had come to be her home?

On August 28th there was nothing left to correct or change or retype, and almost nothing left of her store of energy; her manuscript was ready to be sent off. She typed out the title page, which she always left to the last: *A Light on the Moor.*

Numbly she packaged the manuscript and took it up to the post office. Fare thee well, Charlotte, she said in silence, as it left her hands.

She went home, made herself tea, went upstairs to lie down, and slept the night through.

She awoke feeling ten years younger. The crick in her neck had vanished. She had a lovely leisurely breakfast and then called Simon, as she'd promised to do.

"Marvelous!" he cried. "Congratulations! Bravo! Now, then, a celebration is in order. I shall arrive at seven in dinner clothes, bearing caviar and champagne. We'll go to a place outside Scarborough—it's North Yorkshire French, if you know what I mean, in a Georgian house, but no matter, it's a good place to celebrate. Leave all to me."

It was a gala evening, although Lucia was on a high already, without the aid of champagne or the pleasure of Simon's company. Candlelight and romantic music buoyed her the more.

Simon took a roundabout way home over back roads, driving slowly. Somewhere in a deserted dale he pulled off the road. It was a still, warm, starlit night, and the fragrance of sleeping pastures around them was seductive. He took Lucia in his arms and kissed her in his sweet, lingering way, and with a detached amazement, Lucia observed her automatic arousal, her body responding like a well-trained animal awakening at once from a sound sleep and leaping eagerly to its feet.

"Let's get out of the car," Simon whispered. "I've a rug in the boot."

She suppressed a giggle; she was after all a little giddy. A rug in the boot meant a blanket in the trunk; an age-old, international foresightedness.

"Or," he murmured in her hair, "would you rather go back to Bloodrose House?"

And back to Bloodrose House meant the big bed in the front bedroom, to which he was perhaps not a stranger.

For a moment Lucia held perfectly still while her head, fortunately or unfortunately, took possession of her body, and common sense prevailed.

"Simon, I can't bear to risk buggering up, as you put it, such a lovely friendship."

"*Friendship!*" he protested, and drawing back, wrung her hands.

But it *was* a friendship, for her at least, of the most valued quality, one she'd never had with a man before, one in which the best of herself was allowed to thrive, a fondness based on mutual freedom. Her body's response had nothing to do with such fondness—perhaps little to do with Simon. The pulpy, greedy body, in fact, was an enemy alien in friendship's realm of ease.

"Simon," she wailed, "I don't want to ruin everything by falling in love with you!" But it was such a silly cry that they both had to laugh. "And I never was good," she blundered on, "at casual sex!"

"*Casual!*" he protested again. "My God, Lucia, one thing it jolly well is *not* is casual!"

"Well, then, serious. I don't want serious sex either, and neither, I daresay, do you."

He drew away and sat staring out the open window into the fragrant darkness. "I want to make love to you," he told her finally. "If you must label it, that's *natural* sex. It's what a man must do when he adores a woman. Surely I don't need to tell you that."

"No. But maybe I needed to be reminded." And once more words drove themselves into utterance before she could stop them: "You made love to Helen Farr, didn't you?"

"*Christ!*" His fist struck the steering wheel. "What has that got to do with us?"

And that was how Helen had persuaded him to do her bidding. It wasn't hard, he'd told Lucia, for someone as beautiful as Helen to make slaves of people.

"Damn it," he continued, "you're obsessed with the woman!"

"I expect I've become so. But she left her mark on everyone, didn't she? I mean, everyone was obsessed with *her.*"

He exhaled, leaning back in his seat. "Mark or no mark, let's leave her where she belongs, in the past. Yes, I've made love before. Haven't you? Lucia, I do adore you, but you are driving me *up* the wall."

He turned on the ignition, started the car, and drove on. They rode back to Foxwold in a silence full of distress.

He kissed her again, lightly, on the lips, and took her to her door. She said goodnight in desolation.

The evening was in ruins anyway, but to finish it off she saw across the street a chink of light between Miss Morgan's parlor curtains.

·*XVIII*·

IN golden weather the land paused languidly between summer and autumn, while imperceptible changes were taking place. Days were warm as August, but nights were chilly as October. Morning mists filled the dales. Shorn hayfields turned brown and young winter wheat sprang up, vivid green. On the moors, the mauve of heather deepened to purple. A storing away and bedding down was taking place, both animal and human, but despite this determined bustle the immense quiet of September yawned over the land, a quietness singing almost inaudibly with the thin chant of crickets.

Freed from her typewriter, Lucia went out exploring.

She memorized, took photographs and bought postcards and made notes in a notebook, capturing what she saw, what she heard and smelled in the sweet air, and what she felt, so that afterwards, in New York, she could come as close as possible to returning to Yorkshire.

She felt suspended like the land. It was only a matter of days now before she left Bloodrose House for good. She would go back to New York because it was the only place she could go back to, but she tried not to waste precious time thinking about it. If someone had suggested she extend her lease she would have said it hadn't occurred to her. But in truth, her sense of foreboding wouldn't let her.

During her long respite she seemed to have become more paranoid rather than less so. She had seen neither hide nor hair of Lady Quelling-Steele in weeks; the woman seemed to have retired from the field. But Lucia couldn't believe it was for good. Miss Morgan, chastened, lay low; Lucia hadn't set eyes on her either. Yet as Lucia's countdown approached, she grew more and more anxious about getting out of Bloodrose House without another frightening incident.

It was as though someone, some unknown someone, bided his or her time, brooded, plotted the next more.

Simon, after a few days' silence, telephoned, sounding as friendly as ever and almost as light-hearted. He had patterns and samples of materials, he told her, for Iris's ball gown, and would bring them along to Foxwold the following weekend.

Perversely, Lucia had to admit the game with Simon was better than no Simon at all. She would have to say goodbye to him soon enough; it would be too bad to say it in advance.

Adelaide came to the door one morning with a jar of Olivia's blackberry jam, for it was blackberry season and the glossy black and red fruit grew along the waysides. "We're driving over to Whitby for lunch," she told Lucia. "We thought a breath of sea air would be invigorating. Would you like to come with us?"

Lucia had never been to Whitby, and in fact time spent with Adelaide and Olivia was as invigorating as sea air. She said she'd be delighted.

Adelaide drove her little car with confidence and authority, possessed all necessary maps and travel guides, read them skillfully, and knew exactly how and where to go.

It was a pleasant drive over the moors under a blue sky, and at length the picturesque old town came into view on its headland over the sea, with its ruined abbey and its statue of Captain Cook. They dipped down into narrow streets and pulled up before a shining white hotel overlooking the blue water, the kind of hotel that served an old-fashioned five-course lunch on starched white linen. The drive and the fine salt air had made them all hungry, and they tucked in.

They hadn't seen each other for a good chat in a long time and had lots to catch up on. Adelaide and Olivia said how much they'd liked Lucia's mother, what a hit she'd made with everyone and what a lovely party Lucia had given for her, Miss Morgan's scene notwithstanding.

Lucia hadn't planned to bring the matter up, but now, since Adelaide had done so, she took advantage of it. "What do you suppose Miss Morgan meant," she asked, "by 'She told me to keep watch'? Do you really think Helen Farr would have told her such a thing?"

Olivia, round-eyed, didn't answer. She looked all at once stiffly apprehensive, like someone at table who discovers something she's eaten hasn't agreed with her.

Adelaide's eyes, on the other hand, roved away to the sea-view, her heavy jaw shifting sideways as though she were making up her mind whether or not to equivocate. "Yes," she said quietly, "I do. I think she might have."

"But why? Because she really didn't want anyone to be happy in Bloodrose House after she'd gone? The way Miss Morgan said it, waving her arms about, it sounded ludicrous!"

Adelaide still glared at the sea. "Helen Farr," she said, "didn't like the idea of people being free of her."

"Oh, please," whimpered Olivia suddenly. "Please, Adelaide!" And to Lucia's dismay Olivia's eyes filled with tears.

Adelaide at once reached over and patted her sister's hand. "But we *are* free of her, pet. She's gone. She's gone forever."

"Yes, of course." Olivia bowed her head, blotting her tears with her handkerchief. She looked up and tried to smile but the tears sprang forth again. "Oh, dear. Perhaps I'd better go and dash a bit of cold water on my face. Excuse me." She rose and hurried out of the dining room.

Lucia half-rose. "Shouldn't someone—"

"No," said Adelaide sternly. "If you go to her, it will

only make her cry the more. Leave her for a while. She gets upset whenever Helen Farr is mentioned."

"I'm sorry, I didn't know—!"

"It's not your fault." Adelaide was staring out at the sparkling sea again, her jaw stubbornly set. She turned at last, folding her arms in a judicial way like a schoolteacher about to exercise authority. "You're a very decent sort, Lucia. I trust you. What I'm about to say must be between you and me and must go no further." She glanced over her shoulder to make sure Olivia wasn't on her way back to the table. Deliberately, but without wasting words, she said, "Helen Farr was afraid of plain-speakers like me. Somehow she found out that Olivia had spent some time in her teens at Bootham. In those days they called it a nervous breakdown, and I think they were right; she'd had too much of an aggressive family and a domineering father. But ever so subtly Helen hinted to us both that she could get Olivia sent *back* to Bootham if she chose—and I've no doubt she could with her money and her influence—or get Olivia upset to the point where she'd *need* to go back."

"But that's hideous," breathed Lucia. "Aside from blackmail!"

"It wasn't as clean-cut as blackmail. It was more like a warning. And she used what she knew as a kind of indulgence. She *forgave* one for the family secrets she unearthed, smiled and kissed and brought presents—and kept one in line. Being undisputed queen of the realm was her mania. And so she made a great success of the Festival and the Ball and all sorts of worthy undertakings, and she *was* queen."

"But she must have been hated!"

"She was feared. One didn't *dare* hate her. And being queen was more important to her than being loved."

Lucia sat back in her chair, and now she too looked out to sea. "So good, so kind,'" she murmured. No wonder Cedric believed in the Devil.

"Well, dear," Adelaide boomed, as Olivia took her seat again, "are you ready to walk about a bit?"

Everyone agreed a walk in the sun would be a good idea.

By four they were headed home, quieted by the effects of a big lunch, the sea air, and the scent of heather.

Now Lucia's thoughts returned to the rumor she'd first heard so long ago, that someone might have hastened Helen Farr's death. No one could have been sure that a so-called miracle drug might not work for her, with her uncanny way of coming out on top. No one could have put it past her to go on living, inflicting torment. Someone had had enough.

But it began to seem to Lucia as if *everyone* who'd been in Bloodrose House the day Helen Farr died might have had a reason to put an end to her.

Even plainspoken Adelaide. Even gentle Olivia.

SATURDAY afternoon, keeping his word as he always did, Simon brought the samples for Iris's gown. He stepped into the hall when Lucia opened the door, put down his parcels, and in silence, for he knew by prearrangement that Iris was waiting in the sitting room, took Lucia in his arms. He drew back and looked into her eyes, and their easy fondness was reestablished.

They all three went up to the front bedroom where there was a full-length mirror. Lucia asked Iris if she'd mind removing a few layers of clothing, whereupon Iris stripped off jackets, vests, shirts and so forth until she stood in a white T-shirt and purple bikini, revealing a perfect composition of delectable flesh that made even worldly Simon turn a little pink about the ears. Lucia pinned Iris's frizzy hair up, revealing the girl's pretty neck and ears, and then they commenced to drape her with lengths of satin and brocade in shades of blue, lavender, and rose.

They watched the transformation take place. First there was a look of amazement in Iris's eyes, as if she saw a

150

stranger in the mirror. Next a new little smile curved her lips. Her face changed, and then her posture.

"You were right," remarked Simon to Lucia. "She's going to carry it off. She'll be an enchantress. And if you say *God* to that, Iris, I'll brain you."

But Iris, arching her neck, gave him instead a bewitching smile.

They chose a pale blue satin to set off Iris's violet eyes, and a pattern that carried out Lucia's eighteenth-century idea. Simon promised to order everything from his office and send it along within the week. And presently Iris put all her various garments back on and they went downstairs and Lucia and Simon watched her go off with a new swaying walk which made her look taller and her rag-bag clothing almost chic.

Simon sank down on a parlor sofa and gave way to laughter. "It's incredible. That little fright! And you're just as unfathomable, Lucia, to have seen her possibilities. The female psyche! It will forever be my undoing!"

He jumped to his feet and gathered up his materials.

"I'll leave you now, but you will have dinner with us tonight, won't you? We're only going up to the Arms. No, don't give me that hesitant look, we'll knock on your door at seven. I'll pop in on Will Luddington and see if he'll come too." He paused, his hand on the doorknob. "By the way, darling, what about *your* going to the Ball? It's the night before your lease is up, isn't it? Come with us! All right, I shan't pin you down now, but I shan't forget it." He waved her a kiss and was gone.

He was, thought Lucia, what might be called breezy; perhaps a little too breezy.

She was pondering this when the hall telephone rang. It was Henry Wetherwood, her editor, saying hello from New York.

Immediately her heart began to race so fast that she had to sit down on the stairs. Did he like her book?

He liked her book. (He was never effusive.) He thought it the best thing she'd done. (That was high praise.) Yorkshire had done her good. (It had; yes, it had.) There were one or two minor changes she might consider, and she ran to fetch her copy of the manuscript and go over it with him. They discussed the corrections for fifteen or twenty minutes; they were minor enough for him to execute for her. He then offered her a more substantial advance than usual, and suggested they were considering a promotional campaign. Her treatment of Charlotte Brontë was timely, in terms of the feminist movement.

"I'll see you in New York before long, won't I?" he asked, before hanging up, and she answered Yes, no doubt he would; she would let him know when.

She waltzed back to the study to put away her manuscript and decided to go up to the market square and treat herself to something in one of the antique shops.

Also, she would by all means go to the ball with Simon and his aunts, although twenty minutes ago she'd almost decided she wouldn't.

And that, she supposed, was the incomprehensible female psyche at work.

· XIX ·

SHE was still on a high, Monday morning. Mrs. Berry noticed right away, and Lucia told her about the call from her editor.

"Aye, well," said Mrs. Berry, girding herself in her coverall; calls from editors had little or no meaning to her compared with the importance of good health and good housekeeping, "you've lost that careworn look."

"*Careworn!*" protested Lucia, laughing. "Aye, well, we all need a little pat on the back now and then, don't we, Mrs. Berry?"

"Aye, especially if we've done our job well." And Mrs. Berry bustled off to "turn out" Lucia's study, which she'd been dying to do all summer.

It was true, thought Lucia, finishing her coffee; she'd been careworn, dragging about physically and mentally, trying to finish her book while at the mercy of oppressions large and small—an imminent leave-taking that wrung her heart, Simon's persistence, and a culminating, overriding anxiety about getting out of Bloodrose House, as she had been warned, before it was too late. And yes, one other, to do with Antony Farr, having neither shape nor name.

Today she felt equal to anything. A little pat on the back had filled in all the chinks in her psyche. Simon, too, last night at dinner, had noticed her sparkle and was pleased, although she hadn't the heart to tell him it was the fruit of her own labors, not of his. Perhaps this exhilaration would last long enough to bridge the desolate gap between Yorkshire and New York. And meanwhile she'd try not to over-estimate the ferocity of Lady Quelling-Steele. And stop exaggerating the prominence in her life of Antony Farr.

It was nonsensical; the tears that had sprung to her eyes when she ran from him were nonsensical. Their lives had touched so negligibly that the confusion as to whether or not he was a danger to her was quite unnecessary. Probably she wouldn't even see him again, except at the Ball, at a distance.

She stared out at the misted garden. Yorkshire had indeed been good for her. She had a new fortitude, a new detachment, perhaps a new dignity. It didn't mean she had all the answers, but with this advancement she didn't have so many questions.

Charlotte Brontë had found new strengths within herself, generated by her own genius. A woman didn't have to be a nothing; she didn't have to be queen of the realm either, like Helen Farr. But she did have to be herself, as near as possible to her *best* self, on equal footing with humankind.

Rather than retreat to her bedroom from the rampant Mrs. Berry, Lucia decided to get out of the house altogether. She put on her boots, her raincoat and tweed hat and called over the uproar of Mrs. Berry's vacuum cleaner that she was going for a walk on the fell behind the house.

Mrs. Berry turned off her machine. "Do you think you ought? There's a heavy fog this morning."

"Don't worry. I shan't stray off the path."

She went out by the kitchen door.

It was Lucia's first experience with a real English fog, dense enough to blot out the landscape. But the moist air was delicious, and every wet growing thing—trees, brambles, grass—gave up its own pungency. Branches and leaves and berries made exquisite patterns against the silver mist. It was another world altogether, very still and magical.

The higher she went, the denser the fog became. Now she could see no more than the path at her feet, and she had to watch carefully to make sure she didn't stray off it. She paused a moment, thinking perhaps she'd better turn back.

And as she stood undecided, she heard footsteps somewhere behind her. She was being followed.

The magical shroud pressing around her turned to one of terror.

It's her, she thought, panic pouring through her veins despite her consoling, self-congratulatory thoughts this morning. She wasn't even sure whom she meant by *her*. In this phantom-world of fog it could have been the ghost of Helen Farr.

The footsteps halted. She's listening now, thought Lucia; she's wondering if I heard her.

There wasn't a sound. The fog, all ears, seemed to listen also.

The thudding under Lucia's ribs shortened her breath, but she was afraid to inhale deeply lest she be overheard. Her skin contracted along with her muscles. If she remained there, rooted to the spot, her pursuer had only to come on up the path to her. If she ran, her pursuer could follow the sounds.

For a long time there was nothing but the listening stillness.

Lucia turned, trying not to let even her raincoat rustle. Putting her rubber-soled feet down very carefully, she took six long steps away from the path and stood still again.

She must have been heard anyway. The other footsteps began immediately; slow, purposeful strides.

Lucia stood trying not to breathe through her nose lest it whistle, then tried not to gasp through her open mouth.

The footsteps came abreast of her and stopped again, six feet away. Nothing could be seen in the thick gray mist.

Now, thought Lucia, like an animal trapped in the open, my life depends on my not being discovered. She shut her eyes, as if that might make her all the more invisible.

And suddenly there was a shout, a man's voice: *"Lucia!"*

155

There was only one voice with that imperative enunciation. And without considering whether it was foolhardy or not, she cried, "Is that you, Tony?"

They groped through the fog toward each other and walked straight into each other's arms.

She bent her head, easing her lungs against his chest with labored panting, clutching him by the arms to keep from crumpling to the ground. "Oh, I thought—I thought—"

"Easy now." He held her so that there was no chance of her falling but not tightly enough to constrict her gasping lungs. "Lean on me. It's all right. There, it's all right . . "

She quieted at last and drew back, making a contrite grimace. "Sorry, Tony. I don't know who I thought it was, following me, but I'd no idea it was you."

"I stopped at Bloodrose House to speak to you," he told her, his voice low as if they were in a small room together rather than out on a wilderness of pasture. "Mrs. Berry told me you'd come up here. We were worried about you." He gave her a regretful, half-mocking smile. "My God, woman, how many times must I come to your rescue?"

She sighed, still with her own smile of contrition. She pulled off her hat and stuffed it in her pocket, shook out her hair and brushed it out of her eyes. He raised a hand to her throat and clasped it, and still she had no fear of him. His hand slid up to cup her chin and he bent his lips to hers.

It was a chaste kiss, lasting only a moment or two, with no parting of the lips, but the flood of warmth that surged up and over her made her short of breath all over again. Her response to Simon's kiss wasn't anything like this; it might almost have been that her body mistook Simon for Tony. Weak in the knees, cheeks burning, eyesight swimming, she knew now why she had run from Tony in the past, what the danger was, and why she had better keep on running.

"Oh my dear," he exclaimed, on a quick, husky breath.

This was more than she could withstand, these words, this nearness. His face, the crisp, arched brows and densely lashed eyes, the red-stained hollows of the sun-browned cheeks, were only inches away, and she took a step backwards, closing her lids again for an instant. "Shall we go back?" She gulped. "I mean, what was it you . . . came to the house to speak to me about?"

As if he understood her desperation, he put a brotherly arm around her shoulders and turned her about. "We'll walk, but not back. The fog is thinning, it will burn off by midday. We'll find the rock you like to sit on—yes, I've seen you on it." They were on the path again. "Here, hang onto my jacket, I'll lead the way, I know these fells like the back of my hand."

"Oh, lord, d'you own *them,* too?"

"No," his voice came back to her. "My brother does."

By the time they reached Lucia's rock, the fog had thinned enough to see glimpses of the village, the red-tiled roofs, the tops of trees, and the tower of St. Wilfred's, gradually appearing and disappearing like shoals in the ebb of a gray sea.

And now, seated beside each other, they were more constrained, more formal, as they used to be, and the intimacy of their fogbound isolation seemed to have passed.

"I called this morning," he told her in a businesslike tone, "to leave an invitation to the Ball and to suggest you stay on at Bloodrose House a few days. You won't want to go to a ball the night before you leave."

"Thank you. Perhaps one extra day would help."

"As host I must be at Farthing from first guest to last, so I can't ask you to—I can't escort you myself, you see."

"No, of course not." What was he talking about? She hadn't dreamed of such a thing. "I've told Simon and his aunts I'd go with them."

He started to speak, held back, but burst out finally, "It was just an excuse to see you, Lucia. I can't bear to think of your leaving!" He cut himself short again. For a moment he grasped her near shoulder. Then he removed himself from her, leaned away, arms resting across his thighs. "But the fact is," he said bitterly, "I can't ask anything of you. I can't mean anything to any woman."

She hadn't dreamed of that either. "No," she whispered, not understanding. Tears smarted her eyes, and she blinked them back.

He said, "I'm going to tell you why."

"All right."

"I was going to let you go without telling you, in cowardly fashion, but I can't. I honor you too much." He took a deep breath. "I've never told anyone else. Probably I never shall. Bear with me if I find it difficult."

He said at last, "There was tragedy at Bloodrose House. A tragedy of a marriage, to begin with. Or more precisely, a travesty of a marriage. And a terrible end to it."

Lucia held her breath. She sensed suddenly that Simon was only one of many in Helen's life. Why had Tony endured it?

He told her almost at once.

"I offered her her freedom, begged for my own, long before she became ill. But you see there was something that had happened—with my brother, between Helen and my brother—" (he was finding this rough going) "—which she threatened to make public, if I divorced her. No, I'll not keep anything back from you, not here; I'd trust you with my life. She said he assaulted her." He blew impatiently through his teeth at himself. "Why be finicky? Raped her." Tony's right hand rubbed the knuckles of his left. "George said not. He said . . . it was pretty much . . . the other way round." Silenced perhaps by his own scruples, his own incredulity, Tony came to a halt.

But Lucia already knew Helen Farr wasn't above being grounds herself for blackmail. Simon had undoubtedly fallen into the same trap.

"Poor old George," Tony said softly, almost as if musing aloud. "It drove him right out of England—though not before he'd driven Helen out of Farthing. But he couldn't, or wouldn't, live in the same community with her." Tony's mouth stretched in irony. "Poor Helen. She'd counted on having Farthing to herself."

The lady of the manor, thought Lucia, picturing the blonde, blue-eyed woman in the lily garden.

Doggedly Tony cleared his throat, glaring into the mist, and went on. "It was hard to accept all that I knew of her. Right up to the end, when she lay dying, I wished I was mistaken. How could a woman be so depraved and look so ethereal?"

His hands hung loosely, in despair.

"And then, when the end was only a matter of days, even hours, Jenna told me about a drug that cancer patients were trying in the States, without government approval, and suggested he send for it as a last resort. My blood ran cold. Helen herself had taught us she had the luck of the devil. Even if the drug were quackery, as it sounded, for Helen it might work like magic. Ah, God, Lucia, I didn't want her to live! I asked Jenna if Helen knew about this idea. He said no, he didn't want to get her hopes up. I said, Send for it by all means."

He was absolutely motionless. The chimes of St. Wilfred traveled clearly over the mist.

"Miss Morgan gave her injections for pain, but Helen had painkillers in pill form as well. She'd begun to beg for them because the drugs weren't enough to kill the pain, but Jenna had instructed us not to leave the pills lying about where she could reach them and dose herself at will. At times it seemed inhuman—to deny a sufferer a painless death by overdose. And that same day, after Jenna went off to place a transatlantic call for the new drug, while Miss Morgan was having her brief nap—the only rest she would take—and I was alone in the house with Helen, I gave her a nearly full bottle of pills and filled her bedside water glass."

He was silent so long this time that Lucia thought he'd come to the end of his story. In a sense, he had.

He spoke again, but in a lower register. "She had just

strength enough left to take them, if she chose. She knew that I knew she *would* take them." He was forcing the words out now on steady exhalations as if in a chant. "She whispered, 'This isn't a mercy killing, is it?' She gave me her terrible little sly smile. She said, 'I would have thought your conscience was too great to bear the guilt of murder.' With her own agony at stake, she challenged me! I could easily have taken the bottle back, out of her weakened hand."

Tiny beads of perspiration gleamed on his temples and upper lip.

"But I left them with her. Peg Goodfriend was due to come in in half an hour as she usually did. And Helen died that afternoon, after Peg had left and Miss Morgan had come back on duty."

He was silent again. Then he said, at last, "Helen was right. I murdered her."

She could have refused to take the pills! Lucia cried without sound, clenching her fists. She knew she was dying anyway but with her last breath she put this tragic burden on you!

Yet Lucia sensed to say these things would only add to his suffering.

He folded his arms tightly, hunching his shoulders, as if to protect himself from the cold or to nurse pain. "Jenna certified death due to cancer. If he knew or suspected otherwise, he kept it to himself." Tony added presently, "She left her money in trust to charity, including a large sum for the upkeep of Farthing—another irony, another perpetual reminder—and bequests for the continuation of the Festival and the Harvest Ball."

"And a lifetime legacy to you," Lucia sighed, unable to restrain herself any longer, "of guilt."

With a handkerchief he dried his face. He turned to her, more composed, and now he closely resembled the long, pale, somber faces on the walls of the Long Gallery at Farthing. "I *am* guilty, Lucia, both in my own conscience and in the eyes of the law. God knows I've tried to talk myself out of it, but there's no getting around it. I am guilty and nothing can change that."

Perhaps he did have too much conscience, as Helen had told him, too much honour with a *u*. Yet curiously Lucia admired him the more for it.

He rested his hand over hers as if that touch were all he would allow himself, and then helplessly his fingers closed around hers. "Now I want to tell you this," he said. "You are as different from Helen as it's possible to be. There isn't a particle of wickedness in you. Even that first day when I came crashing up to spoil your picnic I knew I'd made an appalling mistake, using against you an old mistrust. And later, every time I saw you, I learned you were a woman to be treasured, to be explored, to be cherished. Sitting behind you, to the music of those Early English composers, I realized I loved you. I've loved your living in my house; in a strange vicarious way I've lived there with you." He pressed her hand flat between both of his. "If I could, I would keep you forever." He raised her hand to his cheek and held it there, his eyes shut.

He lowered her hand at last and opened his eyes to the unveiling view. "But how could a woman of such sensitivity and spirit live with a man who'd put his wife to death?"

They both gazed over the half-shrouded fields. The mists were thinning. Could I? Lucia asked herself. Would it haunt me too? Or would I think of it at all, ever?

"Now we'll go back," he said.

He drew her to her feet, looked as if from a great distance into her eyes, and then, letting go of her hand, not touching her again, turned and led the way down the path.

Stunned, baffled, Lucia followed.

Helen, living, had had a long reach. Dead, she still did.

THAT afternoon Lucia came face to face with Miss Morgan.

From opposite directions they rounded the retaining wall of St. Wilfred's, Lucia on her way to market, Miss Morgan on her way home. It was bound to happen, thought Lucia, sooner or later.

They stared at each other for what seemed like minutes, although it may have been no more than ten seconds, neither of them able to make a move to step aside.

Then finally, as if Miss Morgan had never threatened her, never been insolent or tried to disrupt her party, Lucia found within her new fortitude the pity she'd withheld before. With a half-sigh, half-smile, she said, "Hullo, Miss Morgan. I'm glad you're better."

The words that came back were uttered so softly that Lucia wondered afterwards if she'd imagined them.

"So he wants you to stay a bit longer, does he?"

They both moved, and Miss Morgan with her thin grin proceeded on down the street.

It wasn't hard to figure out how she'd come by the information. Peg Goodfriend had telephoned Lucia soon after she'd returned from her hour on the moor with Tony, to say that Iris's dress was ready for a first fitting when Lucia could spare the time to help with it, to which Lucia answered she wasn't so hard-pressed now as Tony had very kindly given her leave to stay on at Bloodrose House a day or two after September 30th. Peg must then have made one of her calls on Miss Morgan, and innocently, very possibly in reply to an artful query from Miss Morgan, passed along this bit of news.

In any case, the amicable fitting with Peg and Iris saved a day that had started so well and might have ended abysmally.

·XX·

THE Gainsborough dress took shape. Iris was un-failingly good-tempered, cooperative, and entertaining. Simon came up weekends, and together with Lucia the three of them went into a huddle over every detail of the gown and accessories. A hairdresser was located who would unfrizz Iris's hair and copy the coiffure pictured in one of Simon's art books. Cedric Goodfriend said that with their meticulous plotting they were like terrorists preparing to blow up a bank. Simon replied they were operating on more or less the same principle.

When not working on Iris's gown or the long skirt she was making for herself, Lucia packed for the move out of Bloodrose House to New York. She was thankful to be so occupied, for it was necessary to keep an ever tighter lid on her feelings. She'd had a lot of practice while getting over Julian, but this was harder; then, she'd been getting over something she knew was basically faulty to begin with, whereas now she was saying goodbye to something untried yet full of promise and delight, like a harbor she'd searched for all her life.

Even so there were times, sewing alone or packing or driving over her beloved moors, or hearing an echo of a voice saying, "I'd keep you forever if I could," when the pressure became too great, and a cough that was nearly a sob caught in her throat. And always, there was a dull ache behind her ribs.

How can you feel this way about someone you hardly

know, she asked herself after one of these coughing fits. Someone who hardly knows you? But she felt in some buried abstruse way she did know Tony, had always known him, understood him in her innermost sympathy, as he seemed to understand her. If they were both damaged people, they had in themselves, as he had once said of her, a healing kindness. He was as different from Julian as the genuine from the make-believe. She knew now, too, that her contrariness and fault-finding with Tony were a desperate backing-away from the very opposite feelings, a passionate denial of potential passion. The label of bad chemistry in fact was a protection against the incredible encounter, the hopeless encounter, with a person to be loved wholly and given to without reserve, freeing them both from the past.

> *The human heart has hidden treasures,*
> *In secret kept, in silence sealed;*
> *The thoughts, the hopes, the dreams, the pleasures,*
> *Whose charm were broken if revealed.*

Charlotte Brontë had written that a long time ago, and there wasn't a woman in the world, past or present, who wouldn't understand it.

LUCIA was returning one day from Thirsk when it began to rain so hard that she pulled off the road at the Lamb and Shepherd, a small lopsided black-and-white inn with bright geraniums under its mullioned windows, a favorite of Simon's. It was a pub mainly, but it did serve wonderful dinners to a few patrons, and Lucia was pretty sure the young couple who ran it would be able to produce a ploughman's lunch for her.

They welcomed her cordially and directed her to the little room back of the private bar, where a generous fire burned and the windows looked out over the geraniums into a cobbled courtyard.

And there in a shadowy corner, peacefully reading a newspaper over his lunch, sat Dr. Jenna. There was no one else in the room.

Lucia stopped in the doorway. "Oh, dear," she said unthinkingly. It was Thursday, she realized, his day off.

He looked up, knife and fork poised. "Why 'Oh dear'?" he inquired with a smile.

Right away she knew this was not only a different Jenna from the remote doctor in his surgery, but also from the anonymous man at a party. "You look so tranquil," she told him, "with the room all to yourself. I hate to disturb you." She grinned. "But I'm going to just the same. I'm cold and wet and longing for food and hot coffee."

He put down his knife and fork and half-rose. "Please," he said, indicating the table nearest the fire. "I am happy to see you. I shan't be disturbed."

She sat down and turned to the heat. "When Yorkshire's wet, it's wetter than anyplace I've ever known."

"It takes some getting used to," he agreed, seating himself again.

"Especially if you come from a warm climate," she ventured, inviting him to share something of himself and his background while he was in a sociable mood.

"Yes," he agreed once more, not rising to the bait. "You'll be leaving us soon, won't you?"

She nodded.

"Will you be sorry to go?"

"Oh, yes!"

The proprietor came in then, bringing Lucia a steaming bowl of carrot and potato soup, sliced garden tomatoes and lettuce, a wedge of Cheddar cheese with his wife's homemade bread and butter, and a pot of coffee. Ravenously Lucia devoted herself to the meal, sampling everything at once, while Jenna's liquid purplish eyes watched her from his corner.

She sat back at last and touched her napkin to her lips.

The atmosphere between herself and Dr. Jenna was so different here in The Lamb and Shepherd—relaxed, almost amiable, neither one of them defensive or talking in mystical allusions—that she forgot caution, and suddenly she heard herself asking, "Dr. Jenna, just how sane is Miss Morgan?"

He didn't draw into his shell or seem disconcerted by the question, but gave thought to it, taking a sip of coffee, his eyes hooded. He said, "She knows if there is another public scene, she'll be turned over to the police."

It was too much to hope for, then, that he would give her a straightforward answer; but at least he hadn't coldly cut her off. She studied him, his polished brown skin, his thin lips and hands. "Could Helen Farr control her?"

"Helen Farr was the only one who could control her."

"How did she do it?"

"With rewards," he said softly. His slight smile curved downward rather than upward.

Lucia realized her impulse to speak out with him hadn't been so ill-advised after all. "You mean, she *paid* her to behave?"

"In a sense, yes. But I do not think the object was good behavior."

"Well, rewarded her devotion, then."

"Controlled is the better word. Helen Farr gave her what she wanted." He stared straight before him now, and in the firelight his face had somehow with its grimace become ugly. "Gave her," he murmured, "what she craved."

"Alcohol, you mean? Or . . ." Her own voice fell, and they were almost whispering to each other across the little dark room, " . . .or drugs?"

"Both," he said, as though spellbound. Outside in the courtyard the rain had slackened somewhat but still fell steadily without a sound. He continued, "Helen Farr was Miss Morgan's protector, her mentor, her provider, her—owner. When Helen died Miss Morgan was lost. She is still lost."

166

The fire made a hoarse little pop.

"Do you think," whispered Lucia, "she *taught* Miss Morgan to crave drugs?"

"I have never wanted to know the answer to that."

"But how would Helen get drugs in a village in Yorkshire?"

The heavy glistening eyes moved to fasten on Lucia, yet not as if they actually saw her. If she'd thought he was looking at her personally, she would have been terrified. His thin lips curled back from his teeth. He said, "How else, except through me?"

The log fire collapsed with a sigh.

"And how did she get *you?*"

The contorted face simply stared at her, grinning in agony.

"With her beauty?" Lucia wasn't even sure she'd said this aloud.

He shuddered then, and straightened, and turned to look out into the sodden courtyard behind him.

He turned back to Lucia. "You are an expurgatory person. Perhaps because you are a foreigner, a transient, and one who would not betray a confidence. You have been good for us, for me. Most of us have needed to unburden ourselves where Helen Farr is concerned. Yes, with her beauty. She did not for a moment believe I was without passion." He placed his napkin on the table, preparing to rise.

"One more question, Dr. Jenna, only one, before you leave! Did Tony Farr know about all this?"

He held quite still for an instant. "If he didn't," he said, "Helen made sure to tell him."

The ache behind Lucia's ribs was then almost stifling.

"I did at least withdraw Miss Morgan from drugs after Helen died," said Jenna, "but unfortunately Helen left her enough money to drink on."

He reached down into the shadows under the table and to Lucia's astonishment came up with a violin case. "I must get on to my lesson," he told her, rising. "I play chamber music with friends in York on Sunday evenings. Good afternoon, Mrs. Vail. I am in your debt. You have lightened my burden. I wish you well."

He gave her a little bow and left.

LUCIA started checking and re-checking her doors before bedtime, in these final days.

Even in the kitchen, which looked out on the back garden, she drew the curtains after dark.

·XXI·

FOXWOLD was in the final week of its annual Harvest Ball dither.

Butchers, bakers, fishmongers and wine merchants were all involved in the great occasion, for Mr. Farr liked to delegate the catering to local concerns. The Ravensmoor Arms was again booked solid. And since the proceeds of the Ball went to the Children's Society of the Church of England, St. Wilfred's was undergoing a thorough scrubbing and polishing by a corps of enthusiastic volunteers headed by Peg Goodfriend, after which the schoolchildren of Foxwold would decorate altar and aisles with sheaves of wheat and fruit and vines.

As usual, the post office by day and the pub by night were exchange centers for extravagant rumors. Mrs. O'Bailey, it was said, was going to wear gold tulle over a gold bikini. The Rolling Stones, after a concert in Manchester, were driving up to donate an hour of rock music out of the goodness of their hearts. And there was the perennial report that the Viscount himself was coming home from the south of France to put in an appearance.

There were of course people who went on tending their fields and their animals unmoved by this frivolity. There was also a group of anti-nonsense agitators, temporarily without a cause, who considered picketing Farthing and brandishing placards but couldn't agree on what to denounce. *Ban Balls,* a wag at the pub suggested; and somehow the project fell apart. On the whole, Foxwoldians took everything in stride, as they did the Festival in summer— the frivolity, the rumors, and not least, the monetary compensations.

On Saturday, the afternoon of the Ball, as Lucia was pressing out the copper-colored satin skirt she'd made herself, there was a familiar, peremptory bang of the front door knocker.

Somehow Lucia had known it would come. She stood for a moment, letting the chill of anger and apprehension which had rushed up over her arms and neck subside and getting a grip on herself. Then, turning off her iron, she went out to the hall and opened the door to Lady Quelling-Steele.

Without a word, as if she'd come for a showdown, the lady strode in as before, stripping off her delicate leathers, this time in fawn, tossing them down in the hall and swinging away into the sitting room.

"Now that you're going," she said, inspecting things, tweaking draperies, shifting a lamp, "I'm thinking of renting the place myself for a weekend retreat." She whirled about. "You *are* going, aren't you?"

Despite her intimidating tone, Lucia couldn't help thinking, Poor woman; camping on Tony's doorstep wasn't going to win him either. Lucia held her tongue. A showdown might bring things into the open, but sometimes it was wiser to let the enemy show his cards first.

"The rumor is unfounded, I trust," persisted Lady Quelling-Steele, "that you might be staying on a bit?"

She'd been making inquiries again, evidently at the Ravensmoor Arms. Lucia kept mum.

"Because it would be *most* ill-advised, actually," continued Lady Quelling-Steele, eyes flashing. Lucia's refusal to respond, with the implication that it was none of Lady Quelling-Steele's business, was goading her into behavior even more outrageous than usual. "By rights you should be leaving today. I shall call Slade this afternoon and see about moving in tomorrow!"

Well, perhaps it was time to calm things down. Lucia moved to the window and looked out. Miss Morgan was at work in one of her borders, keeping vigil again. "Lady Quelling-Steele, you know perfectly well Mr. Slade can't give his consent without Tony's approval."

"So you *have* Tony's approval!" cried the wretched woman triumphantly, showing long white teeth.

Oh dear, sighed Lucia. She tried changing the subject. "You realize, of course, that a custodian goes with the house."

"Who? You mean Mrs. Berry?"

"I mean Miss Morgan, across the street."

"Oh, her. Helen's shadow." Her anger, as Lucia had guessed, was so practiced that she could turn it off as well as on, as a child turns off tears. She resumed her tweaking and adjusting as if Lucia's lease had already run out. "Helen always had her vassals, but none so completely subjugated as Miss Morgan." Lady Quelling-Steele flung herself down in one of the puffy sofas, crossed her knees and set her long booted foot to nodding. Having won a small victory, she seemed to feel chatty. "Helen was like royalty, you know, graceful, exquisite, utterly charming. It happened without one's noticing; before you knew it you were following her about, fetching and carrying."

"It happened to you?" Lucia had come to sit opposite her, forgetting for the moment her own fear, a certainty of danger.

Lady Quelling-Steele gave her a stare, as if she found Lucia's astuteness more startling than her question. "I suppose it did, since you, humm, presume to ask. My family were hard up, and she knew I could be tempted with presents and treats I couldn't afford myself. She found poor old Quelling-Steele for me, actually—not rich by Helen's standards but well-to-do by mine. Oh yes, I was hooked by her, too!" There was both savagery and admiration in her voice.

Lucia wondered if Miss Morgan's worship was mixed with the same ambivalence. "How did she enslave Miss Morgan?"

Lady Quelling-Steele gave a shrug. "Oh, that was easy." Miss Morgan didn't interest her. "Something about a bastard child, Miss Morgan's child. It was long ago, when Miss Morgan was an under-maid in Helen's parents' house. Helen couldn't have been more than twelve, but she was a sly one even then. The baby died, and Helen's parents never found out about it, but Helen knew; Helen knew everything that went on, upstairs and downstairs. There must have been something actionable about the baby's death, something Helen could get a handle on. Maybe Miss Morgan did away with the child, I wouldn't be surprised. When Helen told me about it, she let me know she was leaving something out—she had a maddening little knowing smile. Well, from that time on she had Miss Morgan waiting on her hand and foot, and by the time she was older, Miss Morgan was trained to dress hair and sew and do simple nursing, and Helen took her with her wherever she went. Miss Morgan didn't own her own soul."

Lady Quelling-Steele left off with a little explosion of breath. In the next instant she had turned on Lucia once more. "So off you go, back to the States. You didn't catch him after all, did you?"

"No." Lucia was taken too much by surprise to withhold an answer.

"You'll be at the Ball tonight?"

"Yes."

"Is it true that George, Tony's brother, is coming back for it?"

"I really don't know."

With a rustle of silk, suede, and gold bangles, Lady Quelling-Steele sprang to her feet and headed for the hall. "Funny, you know, actually. In an odd way I trusted Helen: one could count on her ruthlessness. But you, my dear, are something else. Too deep for me. Too—*nice*." She uttered the word with the utmost contempt. Hurriedly she put on scarf, coat, and gloves. "There's something for you to figure out with your clever brain: that one can trust the bad but not the good."

She yanked open the door, but as usual paused on the doorstep. "So I shouldn't dally about here," she said, "with or without Tony's permission, if I were you. Go while the going's good, as they say." She turned and looked Lucia up and down. "I can be quite, humm, ruthless myself, actually." With this open threat she moved to take her leave. At the same moment Miss Morgan across the street rose and went indoors.

Lady Quelling-Steele had another afterthought: "I might have been a Helen Farr type myself, if I'd had the money!"

She gave her bark of a laugh and went on down the steps.

PEG, Lucia, and Iris had a dress rehearsal that afternoon in the big master bedroom at the rectory. It went badly. Standing before the oval pier glass in her billows of blue satin, Iris looked stricken. Her face fell.

"*God,*" she began, in consternation.

"Of course you'll have had your hair done," soothed Lucia, seated on the floor where she could adjust the folds of the skirt.

"And you'll have new makeup," added Peg.

But Iris burst out in a wail. "I look like a *freak!*" as if she'd never looked like one before. "I feel like a *fool!*" And breaking into poignant whimpers, she hiked up her skirts and rushed away to her own bedroom.

"Don't cry on the satin!" called Peg, getting to her feet. "I'll go to her," she told Lucia. "It's a dangerous game, isn't it, playing Pygmalion? Are we making a mistake?"

"You mean, we should let her go to the Ball in riding breeches? Peg, tell her I promise, I absolutely guarantee, she'll be breathtaking tonight. Pygmalions we may be, but how can we go wrong with such first-rate material?"

It *was* a dangerous game, thought Lucia, as she walked down the hill; that was the point of the Pygmalion myth and a lot of others. But Lucia had acquired a daring attitude toward change: One didn't have to be stuck with one's troubled self, fool or freak or heart-broken recluse. If the right-hand path led nowhere, it was possible, if one chose, to turn left.

She looked down the street to the facade of the house that seemed home to her, despite the bags packed and waiting to be closed upstairs. Roses still bloomed over the pediment, and bronzed locust leaves tossed shadows over the yellowish stone.

Why, she asked herself, do you not turn from right to left?

But all the while as she descended the hill she was aware that Miss Morgan was again digging in the borders of her front garden, tearing out dried summer annuals.

Stalling, Lucia paused to fondle Bertie, on guard from his favorite lookout, the retaining wall before the Admiral's house, his shaggy little head protruding through the iron railings, his tail wagging within. Delighted, he darted kisses at Lucia's face, on a level with his own.

Someone had found out, Peg had told her long ago, that Will Luddington wasn't really an admiral. One of the bills in the false drawer of the study desk in Bloodrose House might have been submitted for this information. But what had this gentle and gallant man done, or refused to do, to cause Helen Farr to broadcast his secret?

Lucia moved on to her house, hoping Miss Morgan wouldn't notice her or would pretend not to. Or had Miss Morgan stationed herself in wait for Lucia, having spied her going up to the rectory?

As Lucia came opposite and was about to climb her steps, Miss Morgan spoke.

"Mrs. Vail."

Lucia's heart sank. Slowly she turned. "Good afternoon, Miss Morgan."

For a long moment Miss Morgan held her with her pale, brilliant eyes. Lucia noted the flushed patches in the woman's face, an ominous sign. When Miss Morgan spoke at last she pitched her voice just loud enough to carry across the street and no louder.

She said, "You heard her. I did too. Go while the going's good."

There was something intimate and deadly in the reduced voice, aimed at Lucia, something inescapable, like a voice in a nightmare.

There was nothing to say in answer. It was futile to appeal to the woman's reason. Lucia wanted only to get away from her. Heavyhearted, she climbed her steps, went in, and closed her door. She swallowed and stood a moment with her eyes shut.

That's why, she told herself, I couldn't stay on in Bloodrose House if I wanted to. That's why I must go on, to the right, and not turn left. She's won.

Helen Farr had won.

·XXII·

By six o'clock the news was all over town. It was a fact: Lord Ravensmoor had come back. He was at Farthing. Mr. Slade, a pillar of probity, had said so.

In bar and lounge and around supper tables no one talked of anything else. Apocryphal tales of old George's exploits were recounted, with horse and gun, with car and aircraft, with mistress and maid. No one had actually seen him since his return, but some said he hadn't changed a bit; others, resentful of his preference for the Continent, said he'd changed for the worse. One thing was certain: His presence was going to add considerable dash to the Harvest Ball that night.

Simon, checking in by phone from his aunts' house, told Lucia to watch out. George was a cavalier of the old school. Divorced twice, he now played the field with abandon.

"I don't intend to let any old satyrs monopolize you," said Simon. "I'll call for you at nine."

Armed with a little basket of cosmetics, Lucia went up to the rectory at eight.

"They're upstairs," Cedric told her, "engrossed in fol-de-rol."

"There is a time for gravity and a time for fol-de-rol. Isn't that what it says in Ecclesiastes?"

"More or less. And if any two people are going to play God with Iris, I'd choose you and Peg. Go right up, my dear."

The transformation of Iris was already under way. Silken

ringlets, artfully arranged, fell about her face, and tendrils caressed her ears and nape. Seated at her dressing table, she turned her head this way and that. "Maybe it's not going to be such a disaster after all," she told Lucia.

They had experimented with makeup earlier in the week, but Lucia thought it best not to leave the final application to Iris, who out of habit might put on too much rather than too little.

"What we're aiming for is subtlety," said Lucia, drawing up a chair. "A good thing to remember in the future."

Meekly Iris turned up her face, and Lucia went to work.

Peg in black velvet joined them, confirming Lucia's belief that Englishwomen of any size or shape, with or without makeup or stylish dress, have a knack of looking handsome; it was in the character of the face and eyes.

But Lucia knew suddenly that all was not well with Peg—something she'd long suspected. There was a haunted look in her eyes. And Lucia realized they hadn't been alone together in a long time, as if Peg had avoided intimacy and confidences.

"Our sculpture is coming to life," said Peg, as Lucia finished her work.

Iris turned to the mirror. A pearly, long-lashed vision looked back, hoydenishly young, mysteriously mature. The violet eyes widened.

"There," breathed Lucia, "is Iris."

"Oh, child," said Peg.

"Bless my soul," said Cedric, who'd put his head in the door.

"God," whispered Iris.

LUCIA hurried down the hill to finish dressing for the Ball herself.

There was a brilliant full moon, and a wind blew in great sighing surges, like a surf, interspersed with silences. Clouds running low across the sky blotted out the silver light and uncovered it again. It was a night like Lucia's first in Bloodrose House, but the air then had smelled of new life, and tonight it smelled of autumnal decay and dying. With each lift of wind, the locust trees frantically waved their arms and leaves tore loose to go streaming down the street.

There was a restlessness abroad, an uneasiness, transmitting itself to Lucia as the presence of an enemy transmits itself to wild creatures in a wood. Instinctively she darted glances about her, as if someone might be lurking in the shadows. It was a night when spirits roamed abroad, and frightening tales of lost souls on the moor were remembered.

Don't be silly, she told herself, for there was a light in every house on the street, except Miss Morgan's. Lucia hoped she wasn't having one of her spells.

She shivered, hugging her elbows to her sides, and ran up her steps.

The ball gown she'd put together for herself—a copper satin skirt and pink satin sash, with a cream lace top that her mother had brought her from New York—was not as sensational as Mrs. Berry would have liked, but it pleased Simon, who made her turn all the way round and then kissed her carefully on the brow.

"You appreciate the fact, I trust," he said, helping her on with her coat, "that I've been on my best behavior for weeks." He turned her around again. "But I hereby serve notice: I do not guarantee to stay on it tonight."

Lucia grinned. She felt suddenly devil-may-care and fatalistic. "I don't either, Simon," she told him, and they both laughed.

The aunts, swathed in stoles and scarves, were already stowed in the rear seat of the white Mercedes, while the Admiral waited in his old Rover behind them; he was taking his car in case the aunts wished to leave the Ball before Simon and Lucia were ready to go.

The aunts asked right away if Lucia had heard the news about Lord Ravensmoor, and Lucia said she had, and Simon said anyone who *didn't* know belonged to the benighted wasteland outside Foxwold, and with festive humor they set out for Farthing and the Harvest Ball.

THE great house was floodlit from emerald lawn to fanciful chimneys, its tawny stone shining like gold, its tall windows lighted from within.

"We may be a backward country," said Simon as they crawled toward the door in a procession of cars, "but you don't get a sight like that in the States, now do you?"

"Never," sighed Lucia, with a strange poignancy, as if Farthing had some personal claim on her.

But she smiled again. She was determined to enjoy the evening and not to think how close she was to leaving Yorkshire, determined not to use the word *never*.

The great hall was filled with flowers and fruits, arranged in the profligate way of the English, and the thump of a jazz band could be heard from the floor above. Once more they followed the throng up the broad staircase, everyone in evening finery and a-flutter. Not only were the house and decorations beautiful at a Harvest Ball, the music good, the champagne free-flowing and the supper superb, but, everyone agreed, with a wayward Viscount thrown in, the affair was well worth the donation required for a ticket and might rank as the best Ball of all.

They entered the Long Gallery at last and were stentoriously announced, and there sure enough, exchanging a word or two with each guest, was the red-moustached George, a little the worse for wear perhaps, compared to his youthful portrait, a good many pounds heavier, slightly bloodshot of eye and florid of face, but every inch the old-fashioned aristocrat nonetheless. There was an ease about him, perfected to conceal boredom and overlook awkwardness, but at the same time a boldness that would by no means let him conceal admiration for a beautiful woman or hesitate to quell an impudent inferior. He was a man not so much fearless as nerveless—in the RAF, on a horse, in a boudoir. He might be boring himself, thought Lucia, but that wouldn't occur to him, or concern him in the slightest.

He held Lucia's hand warmly while giving her the once-over and drawling something about his brother's good fortune in having so prepossessing a tenant, (he'd trained himself evidently to bone up on everyone and not forget names), and then lingeringly passed her along to his younger brother who stood just beyond him with a glint in his dark eyes, as though old George's heavy charm and Lucia's skeptical expression amused him.

His hand after George's was hard and wiry. His white tie and gleaming white shirt-front emphasized his farmer's coloring. They hadn't seen each other in a week and had had time to think, or try not to think. They looked at each other as if from the opposite ends of a bridge. Their hands touching told them what it would be like to go forward and meet together, and their eyes told them what it would cost. They were going to have to walk forward and past each other.

"Welcome," he said, and somehow she withdrew her hand, dragged her eyes from his, and moved on, began to breathe again.

The aunts and the Admiral were ahead, Simon behind. He caught up with her. He took her arm with an odd, silent tenderness. Had he noticed something? A waiter approached with a tray, and Simon helped himself to two glasses. He touched his glass to hers. "To happiness!" His blue eyes were all merriment.

"Yes, to happiness!" she agreed, determined again to be devil-may-care. But it was a bitter drink.

And then through the gala uproar of conversation, music from an adjoining gallery, and continuous announcements of arriving guests, they heard: "The Reverend and Mrs. Goodfriend! Miss Iris Goodfriend!"

Simon and Lucia faced about.

Good for Iris! She entered like a little duchess, head up, throat arched, bosom lifted, softly blushing cheeks wreathed in dimples. The blue satin dress, tightly sashed, suited her wonderfully, and she glowed with innocent self-satisfaction.

"I don't believe it!" murmured Simon, thunder-struck, and Lucia at that moment had a flash of clairvoyance, so subliminal that it didn't register until later.

A soft, barely audible "Oh!" arose from the crowd, and little subdued hisses sounded as voices whispered incredulously, "Iris!" Lord Ravensmoor, receiving her, held onto her hand so long that the line of guests backed up all the way down to the front door. Lanky young men with hair falling in their eyes materialized from nowhere, waiting to pounce.

"We've launched her into space, haven't we?" said Peg, joining Lucia and Simon.

"Always knew she'd turn into a swan," boomed Adelaide, impressive in plum satin.

"I wish I could say the same," said Cedric. "There've been times when I thought we were parents to some new gender, as yet unclassified—a post-sexual-revolution neuter."

"She's a lovely little lady tonight, sir," declared Will Luddington staunchly, nostrils piping a salute.

"Is she," queried Olivia diffidently, "what the newspapers would call a sex-kitten?"

"You should know," said Simon, putting an arm about her, for she was fetching in pink chiffon, with her spun-silk hair. "You're a sex-kitten yourself."

"Simon, you're being naughty!" And everyone laughed.

"Lady Quelling-Steele!" bawled the announcer, and everyone turned to the door again.

As she'd contrived to do at the concert in June, Lady Quelling-Steele paused in the doorway, giving everyone a chance to see her in glittering gold and silver. She had put sparkles on her eyelids and in her mane of ash-blonde hair, and looked like a mature Queen Titania. She had Rodney, as usual, at her heels, shorter but darker, setting off her blondeness. It had to be said she was well worth looking at.

She might or might not have heard that Lord Ravensmoor had in fact returned. In any case, she put on a marvelous show of amazement. "George!" she cried (pronounced *Gawge*) in a high-pitched caw, and glided forward, hands extended, head thrown back. Gallantly George responded, taking her hands, kissing her on both cheeks and then on the backs of her hands, and at once they were laughing together, like a man and woman, murmured Lucia to Simon, who'd had what was once called a Thing for each other, never consummated but romanticized in retrospect.

Tony was second best again, for now that George was available, Lady Quelling-Steele scarely gave Tony a glance. Better a willing Viscount than a recalcitrant Honourable. She linked arms with George, and since the line of arrivals had dwindled, they went off to the more private bar in the library, leaving Rodney to fend for himself and Tony to take over.

"Has Lord Ravensmoor come back for good?" Lucia asked Simon.

"I doubt it. Antibes is more to his taste. He only comes back to squeeze a little more money out of his bankers. But for Tony, the whole estate would have gone down the drain and Farthing would belong to the National Trust." Simon took Lucia's glass and set it aside. "Come and dance with me."

They went down the crowded gallery past the portraits of wary Ravensmoors to a passage which led to the Armory, another long gallery lined with visored figures in full coats of steel and displays of antiquated weapons. Here, among instruments of slaughter, dancers whirled to sentimental tunes played by a band at the far end of the room, an unbreakable setting for the athletic, or, as the evening wore on, the uninhibited.

Simon was an easy dancer, and they moved harmoniously together. "It's too long since I've held you in my arms," he said.

"Simon—"

"Shh. Enjoy now; talk later."

It was the kind of party that might have been awkward before World War II and couldn't have taken place at all before World War I. Every variety of Yorkshire accent could be heard tonight at Farthing. Merchants and tradesmen mingled with stout red-faced squires and a scattering of elongated nobles. Mrs. O'Bailey, not in gold tulle but in diamonds and red taffeta, unflattering to her ox-blood complexion but worn with splendid indifference, danced with Mr. Buckswick, larger than life in mod evening dress. Dr. Jenna, suave as a plenipotentiary, stood watching. Cedric Goodfriend devised an intricate gavotte with a red-cheeked farmer's wife.

When supper was announced, Simon retrieved Lucia, who had been dancing with George, Viscount Ravensmoor, while Lady Quelling-Steele glared at them over Rodney's shoulder. The crowd had swelled to such an extent that Simon gave up trying to find his aunts and took Lucia downstairs.

The great dining hall had been given over to a long buffet, laid out in immense silver and gilt chafing dishes and platters and lighted by candelabra with pink silk shades.

Waiting in a queue, they watched Iris come in with her retinue of long-legged youths. She had only to raise her violet eyes and make a dimple to set up an agitated stir in the black-clad swarm.

"Cedric was right," said Simon thoughtfully. "She makes her female contemporaries look sexless."

"She told me once," said Lucia, not quite sure why she

was passing this along, "that she loves little kids. She looks forward to having a large family and to hell with Doomsday."

Simon didn't smile. "That's rather sweet, isn't it? Yes, she'll make a charming little mother, and never grow old." He'd lost his own mother, Lucia recalled, when he was three. He came out of his reverie and turned to her. "Heap up your plate, love, and we'll find a corner. I want you to myself for half an hour."

The corner Simon found was in a conservatory, attached by a Victorian Viscount to one of the Tudor wings, a tiled, glass-domed affair filled still with a miniature jungle and its original wrought-iron furniture.

There, when they'd eaten, Simon set his plate aside and hers also, pulled up his chair to face her, his hands clasped on her knees and his eyes bright with their seriocomic twinkle, and to the musical accompaniment of a sylvan spring hidden in the ferns, asked her to marry him.

She knew how fond she was of Simon, and she was tempted then to take him seriously for once. But she was almost as certain that he'd put himself up to this, half-knowing what her answer would be and determined to carry it through no matter what his misgivings. She shook her head. She was flattered that he'd got himself so far out on a limb and in a very tender way told him so.

"Yes," he answered, sitting back, still smiling. "It isn't everyone who gets a proposal out of me." She suspected from the relaxed way he leaned back that he was relieved. "I've a feeling that I may in time acknowledge you superior wisdom." If she'd upset him at all, he turned the tables on her: "Are you in love with Tony Farr?"

Quickly she turned away. The question struck her all of a heap, as her mother's, put the opposite way, had done back in July. The inner hollow, the constricted lungs, the anguish, were the answer.

"Forgive me," Simon interposed at once. "It only occurred to me tonight, in the reception line. And really, he's more your type, more serious, more heroic, a sort of upper-class Heathcliff, or Mr. Rochester, while I'm an inveterate clown, dealer in antiques." He got to his feet, drew her up and kissed her on the lips. "I'll always have a soft spot for you, nonetheless."

"And I for you."

"I know."

"Like two people who've had a Thing for each other."

"Exactly. Come on, we'll go up and mill about some more."

THE English, Lucia discovered, were a lot less inhibited when they let go than Americans. Improvisations in rock and rhumba that in the States might have got people arrested were now taking place in the Armory. What a contradictory, complex society!

George, again dancing with Lucia, squeezed her so tightly that a flush rose in her cheeks. She wished she could convince Lady Quelling-Steele, livid on the sidelines, that it was none of her own doing. Being Lady Quelling-Steele's rival—however illusory—with Tony was bad enough, but with the more eligible, higher-ranking George, might be the last straw. If looks could kill, thought Lucia, and made a note to herself to check on Lady Quelling-Steele's whereabouts when it was time to go back to Bloodrose House.

She soon found herself in the impersonal embrace of Dr. Jenna, where she could catch her breath. Over his shoulder she watched George reclaim Lady Quelling-Steele and lead her into an abandoned fandango. Cedric Goodfriend was mowing a path through the mob with his own helter-skelter inventions, and Simon was now whirling about with the delectable Iris, both of them laughing.

Lucia's subliminal premonition flashed on again and held: Simon and Iris! She could see them as if in a photograph in The Tatler, taken on the grounds of a pretty country house with their babies and dogs. And if Simon, true to form, continued to fall in love now and then, Iris with her sweet good sense would know how to lure him home.

And finally Lucia observed Tony, dancing sedately with Adelaide Ambrose.

"Do you believe in predestination?" Dr. Jenna broke the silence at last. "That all will come right?"

"You mean, even when right seems wrong?"

"Sometimes wrong turns out to be right. We do what we have to do. I learned that from you last week, and it has consoled me. You are unhappy about leaving, but you are made more beautiful by it; therefore something must be right."

"We always talk in riddles, don't we, Dr. Jenna, and yet I seem to follow your meaning." In his mysterious way he obviously followed hers. "You are a good doctor."

He gave her a thin, pleased smile. "That is a compliment I value."

He released her as Cedric Goodfriend approached. For Lucia he toned down his gambols, but dancing with him was still a fairly strenuous business.

"I may not get another chance to tell you this," he said.

Oh, no more, she begged in silence. They were all taking leave of her.

"Your occupation of Bloodrose House has stirred us up in a most beneficial way."

"My being there stirred up a lot of memories."

"A lot of guilty consciences."

Did that include Peg, Lucia wondered?

"Your being there," continued Cedric, "made us realize what we'd allowed one person to do to us. Why? Did we all suffer from excessive pride?"

She looked up at him with affection. From his initial gallop he'd slowed to a mild trot. "Surely not you, Cedric?"

"Oh, indeed yes. No mortal is without sin." A shadow passing over his face reminded Lucia of his expression of terror, weeks ago, in the Snack Bar. "But in the past few months many of us have had to undergo a reconciliation with ourselves, rather than—to throw in a metaphor—go on sitting on our secrets. We've had to face ourselves and humble ourselves. Therefore," and Cedric slowed to a halt on the edge of the dance floor, "I wish you well, my dear, and to the best of my ability call upon blessings for you."

She could only nod, shutting her eyes to dam up the ever-ready tears.

"I'll let you go now." Cedric glanced over her shoulder. "You're about to be spoken for. Good night, my dear." He disappeared into the whirling crowd.

She didn't turn around to welcome whoever was coming. The music had suddenly become crashing, the gyrating couples made her dizzy, and despite the open windows she felt stifled. She fled.

But in the passage outside the Armory a firm hand caught her wrist, and she knew who had followed her. With a look of despair she faced about.

Tony took her in his arms. "I've been waiting all evening to dance with you," he told her. With both arms around her, in a half-dance, half-embrace, holding her close, he moved slowly to the music. "You are utterly lovely," he said.

It was more than she could endure. Desire and despair waged war. She was sure she was going to melt, or collapse, in his arms. "Tony, I need air."

"Yes. Here."

He found a door in the old linen-fold paneling and before she could think twice he drew her into a kind of long service room, lined with cupboards and drawers, clean and empty, lighted by moonlight. Closing the door behind them, he led her down the length of the room and flung open the long windows.

"I used to come here as a lad," he said, "to smoke forbidden cigarettes."

186

They stood side by side for a few moments, his arm around her shoulders, facing the moon-glimmering sky and relishing the silence, taking deep draughts of the heather-scented air.

Then inevitably they turned and crossed the bridge to each other, and a passion like a cataclysm engulfed them. What they'd foreseen dismayingly in each other's eyes earlier in the evening now took place and they lost themselves, one to the other. It was both the result and the resolution of their discord at first meeting. It was the expression, like a floodgate opening, of loneliness and need, a taste of what they might have meant to each other.

When finally they drew back, they breathed as if they'd come close to drowning.

"My love, my love."

"Tony—" Weakly she tried to pull away. He was as unyielding as oak.

"Come to my room," he gasped. "Now. Or let me come to you tonight. I want the whole night with you."

Something went very still within her; the turbulence settled. She answered, "And then say goodbye forever in the morning?"

His arms tightened, and he lifted his face in a blur of moonlight. "God, Lucia, how can we say goodbye?"

"You can," she said, bereft of pretense. "You told me yourself: Helen has a long reach."

His arms fell from her at the mention of Helen's name, but Lucia knew she must say what she had to say once and for all, not only for her own self-respect but for his. "You may or may not have killed her, but she wanted you to think you did, and even dying she knew how to get to the heart of you and make it stick: through your conscience, your ancestral conscience!" Lucia cleared her throat; she must go to the end without breaking down. When Tony tried to speak she stilled him with the pressure of her hands on his arms. "I know the saying, You can always tell a

Yorkshireman, but you can't tell him much. Tony, I have to tell you this."

She spoke softly but she sounded very American, as she usually wound up doing with Tony. Mr. Rochester, Heathcliff be damned; there was no historical romance in this. This was for the present moment. This, again, for the last time, was New World to Old; upstart to Honourable; woman to man. It was the fortitude which tiny, invincible Charlotte had given her.

"Cedric opened my eyes to something tonight. He said my being at Bloodrose House had stirred up a lot of guilty secrets in people who knew Helen, secrets they preferred to keep rather than confess. What you call conscience won't let you face up to the fact that you hated a wicked woman who was your wife, the fact that even if you didn't kill her you wanted to. Is this conscience, Tony? I myself could admit that my marriage had turned out badly, but not that it was I who'd made a mistake. Cedric called it pride: the inability to admit to unacceptable feelings. Tony, beloved Tony, how long are you going to wear this hair shirt?" With these words she brought herself to the brink of sobbing. "All your life? She's dead, Tony, but you are keeping her alive, and you've given up your life to her!"

Lucia ran out of words. She felt as if tears poured down behind her eyes, at the back of her throat. "Goodbye," she managed to say, "and good luck."

She left him, standing as if turned to stone, the moonlight making shadowed sockets of his eyes.

Without saying good night to anyone or looking to see if Lady Quelling-Steele had left ahead of her, she went in search of the Admiral. "Will, I've a splitting headache." That was no lie. "Could you run me home?"

"Of course, dear lady!" He drew himself up, responding to a distress signal. "Fetch your wrap, and I'll be at the door in my car. The aunts are having such a good time they'll never miss me!"

·XXIII·

WILL got out and saw her to her door, and as she fumbled for her key the wind raised a great sigh like a lament.

"Have you got aspirin?" the Admiral asked anxiously. "Take two, and a good night's rest should see you right again. I'll be on hand to help with your bags, though I shall hate to see you go. Sleep well!" He bowed, trotted down the steps, and headed his car back to Farthing.

Lucia went inside and like a robot locked the door. The house was full of moonlight, coming and going like phantoms moving through the rooms, and she turned off the hall light and made her way upstairs—too tired, too empty, to think at all.

At the top of the stairs she gave way, turned, not to her demure Liberty print room but to the voluptuous master bedroom, where she and Tony might have surrendered all their doubts and differences and become one. Like a sleepwalker she went straight to the big taffeta-covered bed and fell across it, face down.

"Tony," she cried softly, in a final goodbye.

And then she knew she wasn't alone.

Someone breathed, close by. Carefully Lucia turned her head, but the moon had gone behind clouds and the room was pitch dark.

Slowly she rolled over and sat up. "Eunice?" she whispered, using Lady Quelling-Steele's first name in the faint hope of placating her. There was an inevitability here too.

Lucia had known for a long time that something like this would happen.

Silently moonlight bloomed in the room again, and Lucia made out the figure standing just inside the door against the wall, saw, too, the glitter of steel.

"You aren't to have him, you know," the woman whispered back, and then Lucia knew it was not Eunice. "You aren't to desecrate this bed, you two."

Lucia crouched, half-turned, in an ultimate terror, a galvanizing of muscle and bone, every hair of her head quivering. "No, I do know that, Miss Morgan. That's why I'm here, alone."

"And don't think you can put me off with your reasonable talk. I'm past being reasonable. It's too late for that."

"How did you get in?"

"Through the study doors. I broke a window. You can change your locks but you can't keep me out, Mrs. Vail." So Miss Morgan had had a key, too, left over no doubt from the days of nursing Helen.

No one would hear her if she screamed, thought Lucia. No one was at home on either side of the house. Her only hope lay in getting past Miss Morgan and down the stairs to the front door. Slowly she gathered her feet under her.

"Don't get up!" Miss Morgan cried out. "Stay where you are!"

"Have you been drinking?" Keep her talking, Lucia told herself.

"Enough to give me courage. She said it was all right. She lets me know, even now, when I can drink, the way she used to. She gave it to me when I was good."

"Miss Morgan, you'll go to prison for this, you don't want that!"

"I'll go to hospital, more likely, and they'll keep me forever, this time. But I have to do what she wants, I never could refuse her. She wants me to kill you, Mrs. Vail."

Lucia's breath rasped shrilly in her throat. Frantically,

pleadingly, she argued on: "Did you really love her, Miss Morgan?"

And once more Lucia's appeal to reason seemed only to inflame the woman. Miss Morgan took a step forward as silver light flooded the room, her rabid eyes shining, the steel knife shining, raised in the same hand that had raised a garden trowel. "Love! What has love got to do with anything? She was my mistress, she took care of me, she was good to me, I would do anything for her." It was like a creed, the words recited in practiced cadences.

"Miss Morgan, was she really good to you? Or did she bribe you, so that she could make a slave of you?"

Teeth flashing, knife flashing, Miss Morgan sprang forwas to bend over Lucia. "Whore! Foreigner! How dare you? Trespasser! How dare you lie on her bed!"

"It's Helen Farr you want to kill, isn't it?"

And at that Miss Morgan uttered a terrible cry, the cry of desolation that Lucia had heard under her window.

Lucia got ready to leap aside. Knowing she might be about to die anyway made her reckless. "You hated her, didn't you? Did she make you kill your child too, did she put that in your head so that she could turn you into—"

"*Don't,*" cried Miss Morgan, lunging forward, "*don't don't!*"

Pain like a sheet of lightning swept down Lucia's arm, someone screamed (herself?), and then she fell back on the bed under Miss Morgan's weight. They had both lost their footing, and this gave Lucia a moment's grace. Unable to raise herself and lift her knife again, Miss Morgan floundered in the soft bed coverings. Lucia could smell the rancid whisky on her breath, and in the intermittent light and dark the grunts and gasps and Miss Morgan's expletives were part of a nightmare. There was a sound of shattering glass somewhere, and that too was hideous.

"It's her you want to kill, not me—"

Then Miss Morgan's forearm slammed across Lucia's

windpipe, silencing her, and her grip on Miss Morgan's wrist loosened, enabling the woman to brace herself on the bed and raise her knife. With her last breath Lucia uttered her last scream, and with her last ounce of strength she threw herself aside in an attempt to roll away. The knife came down along her temple and ear, and rose again, this time surely to bury itself in Lucia's throat.

But a hurricane, a tempest, fell on them.

Miss Morgan was hurled backwards, the knife flying from her hand, and she fell against the wall and dropped to the floor like a rag doll. Lucia was lifted up.

"My God, darling, my God!"

She must have looked ghastly, covered with blood, but her brain and voice somehow wouldn't connect and utter reassurances. In a dream she saw Miss Morgan drag herself up and crawl, getting to her feet, into the hall. Lucia tried to point, but her arm, her hand, wouldn't work.

"Please," her mouth said, without sound, and she passed out in Tony Farr's arms.

·XXIV·

It was dawn when she became fully conscious again. A gray half-dark filled her windows. She was in her own small bedroom. Her arm throbbed. She was heavily bandaged and smelled strongly of antiseptics. The hall light was burning. Was she alone?

Terror-stricken, she called, "Is anybody there?"

Peg Goodfriend appeared almost immediately, in robe

and slippers. "I'm here, love. Dr. Jenna sewed you up beautifully, and you'll be right as rain in no time. He left these pills for you; I'm to give you one if you wake."

"Peg, Miss Morgan got away, I saw her go!"

"No," said Peg, busying herself with carafe and tumbler, "she didn't get away. The police found her at her house."

"Oh, that's a relief! Where—?"

"Lucia, we'll talk in the morning. Take this now and sleep some more. Close your eyes. I'm right across the hall."

Obediently Lucia closed her eyes, and Peg left her.

But for a little while Lucia tried to sort out the fragments of the night before that floated here and there in her brain, scenes of people in evening dress milling about as if in a stylish film of the 1930s. There was an angle-shot of a policeman, viewed from below; he was bent over her, asking questions, and she wasn't sure whether her answers were audible or not. There was a bit of dialogue, too, with Tony. It must have taken place before Jenna and Peg Goodfriend and the police arrived, because she was still worried about Miss Morgan. Tony had hurried downstairs to telephone, and when he returned she was able to drag out a few words: "Please don't leave me alone!"

"I will not leave you alone," he said, holding her. He had ripped up a towel and made a tourniquet for her arm, and was applying pressure to the cut on her temple. "I will *never* leave you alone. Never again. I came to tell you that. I was at your door when I heard you scream. I had to break one of the front windows."

Had she dreamed this?

The pill was making her drowsy. Her arm still hurt, but she smiled, and slept again.

THE fragrance of coffee brewing roused her later that morning. The room was full of sunlight. Her little clock said half-past ten.

Peg Goodfriend in one of her sensible sweater-and-skirt sets came upstairs with a tray.

"You look ever so much better!" she said. "Your cupboards are nearly bare, of course, because you were moving out, but everyone on the street has sent in something. I've boiled an egg from Adelaide and made toast of Olivia's bread and fried bacon from Will. Come, I'll help you into the bathroom to freshen up, and then breakfast."

"And, do you know, I'm starving!" But Lucia found she was none too steady on her feet.

"You're to stay in bed this morning," said Peg. "Dr. Jenna's orders. He'll be in later to see you. And Tony rang, he'll be along after Jenna's visit. I'm to let him know. Oh, and he's sent a man over from Farthing to mend your windows. I'll give him the go-ahead now that you're awake. I was afraid his hammering would disturb you."

"Bring a cup back with you, Peg, and have coffee with me."

Peg went downstairs. There was a knock on the door and voices, but presently Peg came up again with her coffee and settled in a small easy chair.

"Simon came to give you his love," she said. "And he told me to tell you, he did mean *love.*"

"Bless him. See to it, Peg, that he takes good care of Iris."

"Ho ho, you don't miss much, do you? She'll take good care of *him*. She's always adored him, and perhaps a very young wife and very young children will anchor him. They'll manage, and so, I hope, will you and Tony."

Lucia, with sunlight reflecting in her face from counterpane and breakfast tray, turned pink. "Ho ho, you don't miss much yourself."

"My dear, *I* knew you two were in love before you did. And after last night there could be no doubt."

"I don't know what lies ahead, Peg." Lucia sobered. "I'm just thankful to be alive."

"You can thank Tony for that."

"Yes. And Dr. Jenna. And you. You're a good nurse, Peg."

"Oh, I'm an amateur, but I get lots of practice."

Lucia considered a moment. It might be the last time they were alone together like this. Deliberately she asked, "You helped nurse Helen Farr, didn't you?"

Lucia sensed rather than saw the immediate tension in Peg. "I did, yes."

"Did you know she was blackmailing everyone?"

"Yes, I knew." Peg's cup shook. She set it aside and clutched her hands together. "She tried it on Cedric."

There was a long silence, punctuated by a tap-tap-tapping downstairs as the man from Farthing worked on the windows.

"She had ways of finding things out," said Peg.

"Yes."

"I've never told anyone about it, but I would like to tell you, Lucia, because I hope we're going to go on being friends."

Peg turned to the sunlit windows. "Helen Farr found out that Iris is my child but not Cedric's, that she was born out of wedlock. Cedric was an idealistic young clergyman in Wiltshire where we lived, and he loved us both. He married me, adopted Iris, and brought us here to Foxwold. Maybe Helen suspected, because Iris looked so unlike him. At any rate, she must have had someone go and look up the records, and then kept the facts in reserve in case she needed them."

Peg folded her arms tightly across her chest. "It came up when Helen was faced with moving out of Farthing to Bloodrose House, after she'd had that final break with George. Cedric never told me what caused that break and I never pressed him, but it was serious enough for Helen to call on him to take her part, to take George to task, bring the power of the church to bear on him. To the end that it would be George, not Helen, who left Farthing. Otherwise, she made it clear to Cedric, she would broadcast the facts about Iris."

Peg shook her head. "I've never seen Cedric in such a fury. He might have put in a good word for her but for that threat. He absolutely refused. He said if she breathed a word about Iris he would denounce her from the pulpit."

"Hurray for Cedric!"

"Of course he wouldn't have, not Cedric, but he was sick, literally, with anger, and it cost him many hours on his knees in prayer, poor darling. You see, it was his own hatred that horrified him; his first encounter, as he put it, with the Devil in himself."

"He had your support, thank goodness."

"He wouldn't tell me anything!" Tears all at once coursed down Peg's cheeks. "He suffered it alone!"

"Then how did you—"

"Helen! Helen told me! Because she knew from then on I'd try to shield him from such wrath; and from then on she had a hold over me, too!"

"*Would* she have broadcast these facts about Iris?"

"Certainly. Although in this permissive age I doubt that they'd have created much of a sensation. But it wouldn't have been nice for Iris, and it would have racked Cedric. Oh, yes, she'd have carried out her threat. Just as, after Will Luddington refused to dispose of Bertie, she let it be known he wasn't an admiral."

"Dispose of *Bertie?*"

"She didn't like Bertie, and he didn't like her. She claimed he snarled at her through the iron railings."

They both laughed, and Peg wiped away her tears.

The pieces of the jigsaw puzzle were coming together at last, thought Lucia; the puzzle was almost complete. "My God, Peg, any number of people must have wanted Helen to die!"

"Yes," said Peg, very quietly. There was a long hushed moment. "I did."

196

She stirred. "No, don't say anything. Let me go on. It's time. Let me put down my burden."

Lucia held her breath. The man was tap-tap-tapping at the study windows now, where Miss Morgan had broken the glass, but upstairs it seemed very still.

"If there's one thing I've learned from Cedric," began Peg in a low voice, "and I've learned so much!—it's the power of prayer. It works, Lucia, it works amazingly, when one is in need. When I went in to take my turn with Helen, that last day, she was sleeping peacefully with a little smile on her lips. A little smirk, as if she'd put something over, an expression I knew well. Lucia, I sat by her for an hour and prayed she would die. I asked God to put a stop to her. I told him, 'It's high time.' I turned her over to Miss Morgan then, and Helen died less than an hour later."

There was another silence, and then Peg got to her feet. "I'll take your tray down." Her voice shook. "Dr. Jenna will be along soon."

"Peg," Lucia half-whispered, "everyone must have prayed that same prayer!"

"God forgive us!"

"Peg, even Miss Morgan! Oh lord, I almost forgot about Miss Morgan. Is she really in custody?"

Peg grasped the tray. "No, dear. Not exactly."

Lucia paled. "In hospital then? I hope?"

Peg shook her head and looked Lucia in the eye. "No. She's dead. The police got to her house as quickly as they could, but it was too late. She'd hanged herself in her cellar."

With a little low cry Lucia dropped back against her pillows. They'd all paid dearly for hating Helen Farr.

Miss Morgan had paid with her life.

DR. JENNA arrived at noon, looked Lucia over thoroughly, and told her she might get up for an hour or so but not to try to dress. He would come in again tomorrow. He gave her an odd little smile when he left, as if he thought she'd created enough excitement for a while.

His medication was making her drowsy again.

Peg telephoned Tony as she'd promised and suggested he come over later in the afternoon when Lucia had had a nap, insisted to Lucia that she would return to help her into a robe and slippers, and went off to attend to her own family.

And thus it was that Tony, letting himself into Bloodrose House at four o'clock, found Lucia in a becoming blue robe sitting with her arm in a sling on one of the small sofas before a warm log fire, downstairs.

Carefully, so as not to jar her, he inserted himself into the available space beside her and took her free hand, his circumspect actions very much at odds with the emotion in his face. "You do look better," he said. "Thank God. What a sight you were last night. I thought she'd half-killed you."

"You were just in time, Tony. She would have killed me."

He drew back then, frowning, and closed both his hands over hers. "Lucia, what you said to me at Farthing last night was all truth. No, wait. Up to that point I would indeed have bade you goodbye in the morning, not in spite of my love for you but—due to my arrogant, misguided conscience—because of it. But when you walked away from me at the end of it, out of my life, I knew, finally and incontrovertibly and desolately and forever, that I couldn't, I could not, let you go!"

She shook her head in compassionate agreement.

He said, "When I couldn't find you at the Ball, I followed you here to ask you to marry me." He set his teeth as though laying himself open to utter demolition. "Lovely, honest, mettlesome girl, will you? Would you consider it?"

He was so in earnest, so vulnerable, his feelings so evident, that she hastened to put his mind at rest. She had never smiled a more radiant smile. "I most certainly would," she said.

He looked into her eyes with wonder. Since he couldn't embrace her with her arm in a sling, he took her face in his hands and kissed her lips, long and firmly, long and softly; experimentally, then purposefully.

"But Tony," she said, when they drew back to catch their breath, "I don't know anything about farming!"

He broke into a rare laugh. "Why should you? I don't know anything about writing novels. One farmer and one writer living in the same house may be much better off than two farmers or two writers. We've both been through enough to learn it's what we are that matters, not what we do. Will you mind living in England?"

"Will you mind being married to an American?"

For answer he took her face in his hands again, and there were several moments of rapt silence. "Lucia," he murmured at last, "this will be more of a first marriage for me than a second."

"For me, too. But a happier second because of an unhappy first."

He got up, in order to concentrate on practical matters, and, handsome in a gray Sunday suit, stood before the fire. He said, "Jenna tells me your arm will be healed in two or three weeks. That would give us a decent interval in which to post the banns and arrange a small wedding at St. Wilfred's, do you agree? Is that too impatient of me? Would your mother come?"

Lucia, smiling her unreserved smile, nodded and shook her head and nodded.

"You'll stay here at Bloodrose House, if that's agreeable to you, and think about where you want to live after the wedding. I took the liberty of discussing my intentions with George. He greatly approves of you. He wants to invite you to Farthing himself before he leaves for Antibes on Wednesday."

"So soon? What about Lady Quelling-Steele?"

"She'll turn up in Antibes too, you may depend on it.

George will cope. He hasn't managed to remain disengaged all these years for nothing. The fact is he's not in good health. He wants to turn over Farthing to us to do with as we like. If we like."

"Let's live here a little while at least. We owe it to this kindly house to give it some happy memories."

He didn't laugh. "There you are," he said softly. "That's what I cherish in you. My God, darling, if it weren't for those cuts and bruises—"

"Yes, I know."

"Yes. Well." He brought himself back to business. "There's one last thing to attend to before we have tea, which I've brought in a hamper, packed by Mrs. Clay with her blessings." He reached in his pocket and drew out a slip of paper. "One last thing concerning the past, and then we can close the book. Peg told you about Miss Morgan's death? Right, I asked her to, when you were feeling better. Miss Morgan left a note. The police aren't going to make it public, but the chief constable wanted me to have a copy. I'll read it to you.

Mrs. V. was right, I must have hated Mrs. F. She made me flush some painkillers down the toilet that Mr. F. gave her so in case she died he would think it his fault. But Dr. J. told me he was going to start her on a new drug. I don't know what came over me. I injected air in her vein instead of morphine. God have mercy on my soul.

Lucia bowed her head. "Oh, Tony." It was the last piece of the puzzle.

"Amen to her prayer," he whispered. He tore the paper into bits and threw them into the fire. "Would you like some iced champagne before tea?"

She looked up, startled, breaking again into a smile. "Do you happen to have some on hand?"

"In fact, I do." He went out to the hall and came back with a bottle wrapped in linen and two goblets.

He removed the cork neatly, filled the goblets, and returned to Lucia's side on the sofa. They looked at each other and smiled for the present moment, and then, quite gravely, they drank to the future.